GHOSTS, GOBLINS
& HAUNTED CASTLES

Written by Jaroslav Tichý

Illustrated by Marie Preclíková

TREASURE PRESS

First published in Great Britain in 1991
Designed and produced by Aventinum for
Treasure Press, Michelin House
81 Fulham Road
London SW3 6RB

Copyright © 1991 Aventinum, Prague
Copyright © This edition by
Reed International Books Limited 1991
Translated by Vladimír Vařecha
Graphic design by Aleš Krejča

ISBN 1 85051 623 5

Printed in Czechoslovakia by Svoboda, Prague
1/20/11/51-01

GHOSTS, GOBLINS & HAUNTED CASTLES

Contents

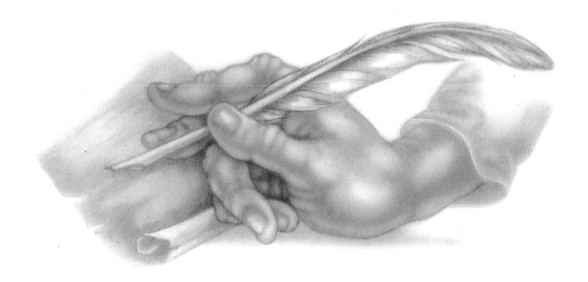

The Giant Spinning Wheel on Geissberg Castle

In the days when bees in Switzerland built honeycombs as high as city walls, and children plucked cherries from the trees as big as apples, there were some lords of the castle who also forgot that they ought to stop growing. One such family of giants, a widower with two sons and a daughter, took a liking to the countryside around the village of Villigen. On top of the hill Geissberg, above the slopes of the vineyards which towards autumn make the valley where the rivers Reuss and Aara join, shine like gold, they built a castle. It must indeed have been a pretty sight for the villagers in those days to see the two giant sons with their giant Daddy on the building site throwing boulders from hand to hand as if playing a ball game!

At last the castle got its roof. It was indeed an edifice worthy of giants: its mighty ruins crown the rocky top of Geissberg to this day!

'A goodly castle,' said the father of the family and the lord of the castle when he saw that everything from the well to the sheet-metal vane on the top of the tower was ready. 'Thoroughly built and a lovely sight to boot. But what shall we do if one fine day an enemy approaches with an intent to take the castle by storm? We shall have to possess a goodly supply of missiles ready for our catapults so we can give him a proper welcome and something to remember!'

'I saw some pretty little stones on the river-beds,' said the daughter, Hilda, all of a sudden. 'About as big as a man's head, they were. I believe they would do for our slings.'

'Oh well, those walks of yours along the

rivers are of some use after all,' said the lord of the castle approvingly. 'The boys and I will go down to the valley and get some tomorrow.'

The whirlpools of the Reuss and the Aara were too dangerous even for the best swimmer amongst the Villigen inhabitants. However for the Geissberg giants it was but a pleasant walk. The Father and the sons each uprooted a well grown firtree in the forest so as to have some kind of a staff for the journey, and having descended into the valley they set off along the river-bed as if it were a paved road. The water barely reached halfway up their shins and wet not so much as the edge of their tabards!

Meanwhile, the little sister, who had stayed at the castle, began to spin thread on her giant spinning-wheel. This she wove into the fine fabrics she fancied. The spinning-wheel was so enormous that it could easily have driven a big mill. A whole fir stem had been used to make the distaff and the spindle was hewn by Hilda's brothers out of a boulder of granite left over from building the castle. Is it any wonder that the buzzing of such a spinning-wheel could be heard all the way down into the village?

Every time the Villigen citizens heard the sound they scowled in anger. They held no love in their hearts for Hilda of Geissberg, for she played with their village as if it were a pile of toys. She was a maiden full of whims, and spoilt like a true lord's daughter. She knew how to worry her father and her brothers with tricks that even a mischievous boy would not think of. Thus she once caught the tower of the Villigen church in her fingers and set it down behind the village just like a feather.

'Leave the village down below in peace, daughter, have done with it!' raged the Father and lord of the castle at the dinner-table one day, and banged the table with his fist till the dishes which were as big as vats jumped up. 'Even the reverend local vicar has complained to me about you!'

Hilda, however, did not heed the clergyman's

or her father's chidings. A few days later she laid the vicar's coach on to her palm just as the reverend gentleman was about to drive away into the town to visit the bishop — and let it ride down the hillside like a toy-cart! The vicar could only wring his hands in despair!

On another occasion, she became entangled with a village wedding party. She had hardly turned round once or twice among the dancers, than the next moment bride, bridegroom and all the wedding guests were floating above the roofs of the cottages lifted into the air by the whirlwind raised by the ogress's wild dancing. Although they made a soft landing having dropped into a big haystack on the common, the whole wedding was spoilt.

'My only son is getting married, and such a horrible scandal,' lamented the mayor, whose son it had turned out was the bridegroom. He was right: the young man's head was sticking in the hay and he was shaking his Sunday best boots in the air.

'This is something we can no longer let go unpunished, neighbours,' said the angry Villigen citizens when they gathered for a meeting of the town council. So they sent a letter up to Hilda urging her at long last to give up ridiculing their elders.

'But I am not at all to blame, my dear peasants,' shouted Hilda from the window of the castle tower after reading the letter. 'All I wanted to do was to dance a little jig on the common in honour of that wedding of yours. I would give my heart and soul for a bit of dancing, so who can hold it against me?'

All this gave to rise a lot of bad blood in the village, a feeling which remained for a long time. Yet even that was not the worst of her pranks.

One sunny day she thought of having a little fun by the river Aara, the way boys will sometimes play on the edge of a brook. She could think of nothing better than to hollow up rills on the river bank. It was indeed a magnificent

9

sight to watch the river water rolling through the ditches into the nearby meadows and in the end flooding the whole valley!

This was of course beyond a joke, and the people of Villigen lost patience with the ogress. All their roads and meadows were under water — and the hay harvest about to start! The neighbours waited till the lord of the castle and his sons set off again to look for stones in the river and having armed themselves with pitchforks and scythes they hurried up to Geissberg to teach the young lady a lesson.

The road rose steeply, and the poor peasants not only began to lose their strength but their courage as well. When they reached the closed gate, however, one young fellow took heart. He lifted a stone and flung it into the gate for all he was worth.

For a moment all was silent, then, something happened to cause all the people of Villigen to lift their faces up towards the tower. From one of the windows echoed a buzzing as if a cloud of may-bugs was flying across the mountains. The buzzing grew and intensified into a menacing roar: it was Hilda of Geissberg in her chamber turning the spinning wheel with ever increasing ferocity. The armed villagers had outraged her mightily — and the thump upon the gate was the limit!

'So much to-do and uproar for a bit of water which had overflowed the banks into the meadows — before long I won't be able to make a little pond down by the river Aara — and with this tremendous heat wave as well! Those boors of peasants have no sense of humour!'

As she turned over in her mind how envious of any pleasure they were, her anger began to rise to a white heat, and she turned the spinning-wheel faster and faster. The stone spindle was turning with ever greater fury, the buzzing and roar becoming a deafening howl and suddenly a terrific bang divided the air like a flash of lightning. The turning spindle flew from the spinning-wheel out through the window and right over the heads of the people of Villigen, dropping into the Aara with such a thump that the water in the river hit the church tower clock.

The poor peasants of Geissberg were completely overwhelmed, and their courage left them. They ran back down the hillsides into their cottages wishing all this had been just a horrible dream.

Yet, it was no dream, not at all, for to this very day when the water level drops in the Aara River you can see in it a big boulder in the shape of a spindle. It is the very boulder that Hilda the giant flung out of the open window of the tower of Geissberg Castle.

Ragnar and Svanhvit

The ancient city of Uppsala had been the seat of the Kings of Sweden from time immemorial. Even before they built the fortified palace which is to be seen to this day, there had been a castle standing upon the site. Though more like a mere stronghold, it still was a ruler's seat. According to legend it was King Hunding who reigned there in days gone by. It so happened that one day the said King Hunding received an unexpected message that his old friend Hadding, King of Denmark, had met with a sudden death.

'You were closer to me than my own brother, dear friend. What better way of honouring your memory than by a proper wake?' said King Hunding, as though his dead friend was there to hear. 'Bards shall sing of your deeds of valour and the halls shall resound with the praises of all who knew you.' The king also thought that the feast should be more than plentiful in order to mark such dignified commemoration ceremony, so he set out to inspect the stores of food and drink. Just as he was descending the spiral staircase into the cellar where beer was ripening in a gigantic vat he stumbled over a loosened stone, fell headlong into the vat, and was drowned.

Such was the death of a man who had been lucky enough to escape from so many perils and passed through the fire of so many battles. This was, indeed, not a death worthy of a King, and as it turned out later, quite unnecessary as well. For Hadding, the King's friend, was safe and sound, and the news of his death entirely false.

However, misfortune comes on wings and departs on foot. When Hadding learnt that King Hunding had actually drowned on his account, sorrow and reproachfulness would not let him sleep.

'I cannot live on in this world, dear friend, burdened with such a guilt. I will join you in Valhalla, the seat of the highest god, and there, in the palace of dead heroes, we shall drink together many a cup of a rare potion, with which

Odin has pledged stalwart hearts for ages!' said King Hadding, and thereupon he put a noose round his neck. Yes, indeed, the faithful Hadding hanged himself in despair.

The lands of Sweden and Denmark were overcast with sorrow over the passing of the two noble friends. The only one who was overjoyed was Thorilda, King Hunding's widow and step-mother of his sons, for she had long desired to rule the castle by herself. Now that her husband was dead, the only obstacles in her way to this goal were her stepsons, Ragnar and Thorald. From that moment on she thought of nothing but how she might get rid of the two boys once and for all.

The two young men, like their father, had courage in their blood. From their mother who had died before they grew out of children's shoes they inherited a good heart that had no

power to see through any villany. So when Thorilda started complaining that the King's herds were diminishing, the brothers saw no subterfuge in this and sought to help her. Obeying her wish they would go out with the cattle to pastures far and near dressed like shepherds so as to save their noble attire.

It did not occur to them in the least that what their stepmother desired was that they should lose their lives in some remote spot. Pastures and meadows were the haunts of ghosts and evil spirits in those times — but that was something the young princes took no heed of.

However, reports of Thorilda's evil plans soon spread among the dead King's subjects, and many of those who heard them pressed their lips bitterly and clenched their fists. Even while the King was still alive, Thorilda delight-ed in making people feel her cruelty; what bad times were in store for all when the Queen had got rid of the Princes and ruled the Kingdom on her own?

Among those who learnt about the Queen's base intentions was the golden-haired Svanhvit, daughter of Hunding's late friend Hadding. She lost no time in calling together her maidens' retinue, saying, 'It is not enough that two good friends of matchless courage are dead. Are the two young princes to become victims of evil spirits as well? My loyal companions, let us set off for Uppsala this very day and warn them! Let us save Ragnar and Thorald!'

There were no more lovely maidens in the whole of Denmark than the golden-haired Svanhvit and her nine friends. Nor would it be easy to find any who were more daring. Their most favourite pastime was to dash through the countryside on horseback and practise archery. Many men were envious of their strength and agility; should a fight ensue, who could tell whether victory would go to the men!

When the maidens crossed the Swedish borderland there was still a good way to go to the Uppsala castle. However, Ragnar and Thorald had happened to wander with the cattle just on

to the border meadows that day. These were the
pastures which were said to be the favourite
haunt of spectres.

Svanhvit knew this too but if she wished to
get to Uppsala there was no choice, whatever
the cost.

When the brothers saw the maiden riders in
the distance, their red shields shining like pop-
pies, Ragnar said to Thorald:

'It seems that the Valkyries are coming —
those fairies who guide the souls of fallen
warriors to Valhalla. You stay with the herd,
Thorald, and I will ask them whither they are
riding; as a King's sons, this is something we
should know.'

When Svanhvit's companions saw the young
man in a shepherd's clothes they wished to get
down from their horses and ask for a drop of
fresh milk from the cows which the young men
were grazing nearby. Svanhvit gestured to them
not to dismount. 'Can't you see with what fury
the black clouds are racing across the sky?
Those are witches and fairies with eyes of spar-
row-hawks and buzzards which can see even
a little mouse from their height. A man on foot
would be an even easier prey to them! They
have the power to turn in a moment into a pack
of werewolves with fangs and claws with which
to tear their victim to pieces. Look how they
assume a thousand forms in the sky!' said Svanhvit pointing to the wind-driven clouds.

'And the slyest of them then assume the likeness of men,' she added in a voice full of distrust when she looked at Ragnar.

'Indeed, I am no ghost,' said Ragnar having
approached to within a few steps of Svanhvit's
steed. 'I can't even tell how I wandered off my
track to this remote meadow.'

Now that Svanhvit could take a close look at
the young man's blue eyes, she saw they had the
colour of the eyes of the dead king Hunding.

'You are a man of royal blood, not of the
blood of serfs,' she said firmly. 'The brightness
of your eyes as well as the beauty of your face

give you away. Therefore flee as fast as you can from these parts, and take hidden paths in your flight; the monsters that haunt the air and the wind above our heads are searching for a noble prey. Woe betide the nobleman who is not in the saddle of a fast horse!'

'Oh bother,' said Ragnar to himself, 'now that she had recognized me for what I am, what will she think of my coarse shepherd's rug?' He was overwhelmed with shame because of his attire which did no honour to a royal heir, and answered, 'You are wrong, maiden! I come from the blood of the poor, and have been living in poverty since my young days, but that doesn't mean that I am a coward and a boor. Even an attire soiled through hard work can hide a brave man. I am afraid of no man in the world, not even of the queen of spectres or wills-o'-the-wisp or night-riders racing across the skies. Nor do I fear the king of elves though he may be the slyest of them all. I am ready to fight them even with my bare hands!'

Svanhvit listened to Ragnar's words as though lost in a dream. The resolve in his look aroused affection in the maiden's heart. Now she was all the more concerned about his safety.

After a brief reflection she drew from the sheath by her horse's saddle a double-edged sword whose hilt was decked with silver and amber, and bent down to put the weapon into Ragnar's hands.

'If unarmed you dare to challenge monsters more ferocious and cunning than ten human warriors, you possess the courage of gods; never have I heard of a man more daring. But courage ought to be allied to a sword and the sword should be equal in strength to that of the arm that wields it. Here take what is your due: the sword of Hadding, my father, who had many times fought side by side with King Hunding in defence of our countries.'

Thereupon Ragnar realized that the maiden he had taken for a Valkyrie was the daughter of his father's closest friend. Suddenly he felt

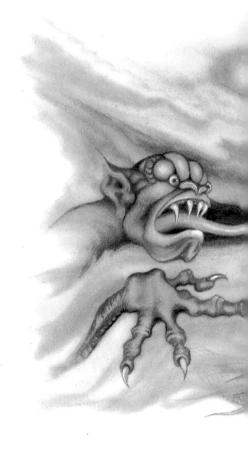

affection toward the noble-minded maiden. He accepted the sword and, kneeling down, kissed its hilt. Then he rose to all his vigorous height and cut the air with the blade till it rang out and its whetted steel shone like a flash of lightning.

The spectres flying through the air took this for a challenge, and began to set about Ragnar. They had flaming mouths, thighs and arm-bones, and claws instead of fingers. Skulls on webbed wings rushed from the moors and forests, and goblins with limbs gnarled and twisted like tree roots tried to make Ragnar fall to his knees.

The whole night long Ragnar fought with the monsters and he would never have won without Hadding's sword. It was then that he realized its magic power.

When the veil of mists rose in the morning and dispersed in the cloudless blue sky, the

fighting stopped. At long last Svanhvit's companions were able to dismount and rest on the grass. Svanhvit sought the exhausted Ragnar to dress his wounds.

'Look there,' she said suddenly and pointed out a spot in the grass where something glittered. Ragnar approached it, and what he saw was a tiara set with precious black stones and a bracelet made of twisted little snakes, and a ring with a mysterious symbol. He knew them only too well, for the jewels belonged to his stepmother! He looked farther, and among the most hideous witches lying dead beside the other slain monsters he recognized Queen Thorilda! She had come flying through the air on a black horse all the way from Uppsala Castle to lead the battle against the King's sons.

Svanhvit told Ragnar and Thorald to have all

the dead monsters burnt to cinders. 'Believe me,' she said, 'they would rise as though newly born at the next full moon. You would never be rid of their mischief!'

No sooner had the fire burnt out than the royal brothers and Svanhvit with her suite of maidens set off for Uppsala Castle. The square tower of blackened oak beams looked bleak from a distance but when they got closer they saw that the castle galleries were crowded with overjoyed men and women waving whatever they had at hand: shawls, caps, and hastily sewn together banners. The news of Ragnar's victory had run before the hero's return.

For three days and three nights did the people celebrate Ragnar's coronation, and this was all the more glorious, since the new King got engaged to his beloved Svanhvit at the same time. Before long she became his wife and the new Queen of Sweden.

18

Finn and the Big Man

In times of yore a man called Finn was living with his courtiers on the south coast of Ireland. He built a castle by the sea so strong and fine that remnants of its walls have been preserved from those ancient times down to this day.

It was there that Finn lived and defended the country with his men whenever an enemy attacked it from the sea. The invaders would come sailing in their fighting skiffs intent on conquering the Green Isle. The borough of Ventry could give the best account of this, for it was near Ventry that a terrible battle was fought once, and Finn and his men were hard put to it to carry the day.

For some months, however, the enemy had made no appearance and so Finn was able to enjoy his beloved fishing in peace. One day it happened that he was seized with a desire to eat roasted limpets. As bad luck would have it however, not a single one got stuck in his fish-trap.

'Well, shrimps and prawns will also come in handy when there is nothing bigger to eat,' he said to himself. He tied the boat to a pole, and just like any shepherd who got hungry while grazing his sheep he set out along the beach in search of some.

Finn caught a handful of limpets just big enough for a little snack before lunch, made a fire on the beach, and started to roast them. The sea looked calm that day, and as Finn took pleasure in surveying the vast expanse he did not fail to take the bay of Ventry Harbour into his ken. It was here that he spotted something that one cannot claim to be an everyday sight.

A skiff with a large purple sail was heading for the shore with no one on board except one single man. He was much taller than Finn and clad in the most expensive armour that Finn had ever seen in his life. That he was not just a simple ordinary man was clear at first sight.

'In the end he will catch me at the fire with these limpets like some vagabond with nothing better to eat,' Finn thought to himself. 'After all is said and done, I am the lord of the castle.'

He did his best to throw all that was left of the limpets back into the sea, but the Big Man was too near for that. He had just stuck the point of his sword into the deck and gave a mighty leap to the shore. As he landed the earth nearly trembled.

'Tell me where here do Finn and his men live?' he thundered at Finn with straddled legs high and strong like pillars.

'They live above there,' said Finn pointing towards his castle. 'And I am one of his men.'

'Finn and his men have a great name as brave warriors. Is that so?' the knight went on.

'So they have. To be sure, they come from the house of Fianna, the bravest in the whole of Ireland,' said Finn, 'they do indeed live up to their name.'

'All right, all right,' growled the Big Man. 'I am a warrior from the Land of Big Men. There is a horrid monster at the bottom of the largest of our lakes and now he has got the idea of taking our King's daughter for his wife. There is a prophecy of the King's soothsayer that the only man who can bring the monster to his senses is Finn of the land of Ireland, and so my King has sent me to try and find that valiant man.'

'Oho,' Finn thought to himself. 'They want to lure me out to fight some monster and to arrest me.' So he said aloud, 'Finn won't come with you alone, his men would be anxious about him.'

'His men can be calm,' laughed the giant

aloud. 'I will undertake to protect Finn. For I myself am protected by all possible charms and no weapon on earth can hurt me. If you wore a sword you could see for yourself!'

'I have something of the kind at hand,' cried Finn. 'When I roast a wether's haunch over the fire I use this cutter to put the pieces straight into my mouth,' and he drew from under his cloak his famous sword which he had used to repel many armies of intruders. He swung it over his head and hacked at the Big Man's shin for all he was worth. Try as he might he could not reach any higher.

'Oh, oh,' cried the knight and started skipping on one leg, and rubbing the spot where the sword had hit him. 'If all Finn's men are as strong as you, then you have something to be proud of. Though I am protected by the charm I did feel the pain.'

'I must confide something to you,' said Finn in a mysterious way. 'As to strength and growth, I am but a child compared with Finn and his men.'

The giant did not seem to mind that in the least. 'Can you finally show me the way to get to Finn's castle?' he thundered and did not look as if he was going to wait long for the answer.

So Finn showed him the path they had used when carrying stone to build the castle. It was a roundabout route, but on the other hand it was fairly wide and the Big Man set out along it with a will. This was a road upon which he really did not have to mind his step!

Meanwhile, Finn climbed up to the castle taking the short-cut. He went straight into the kitchen where Gráinne, their house-servant, was getting the dinner ready.

'Give over your cooking, let go the dishes, let go everything on earth, dear Gráinne, and listen to me carefully! There's a giant warrior coming here to see me but I am in no mood to receive him. I will hide in the flour-box over there, and should the warrior still manage to catch a sight of me you'll tell him that I am your just new-

born son; perhaps he will leave a baby in peace.'

Gráinne, however, did not fancy the idea, 'And what about your red hair, Finn, what about your beard? I've got it, I'll cover your head with my embroidered nightcap and your chin with a bib my daughter used when she was little.'

'My head is used to a helmet from which the sun reflects lightnings into the eyes of terrified enemies. Do you really believe that I can put it into a woman's nightcap?' cried Finn and gave her a look that sent her rushing into the pantry to fetch a blanket to cover Finn from head to foot in the box. Before she got back, however, Finn was already lying in the box with the nightcap on his head.

Before long a sound like the rolling of thunder shook the castle: it was the mighty warrior stalking through the lower hall, and, not know-ing his way about the labyrinth of the castle corridors, burst right into the kitchen.

'Is this the castle of Finn whose courage is renowned even across the sea?' he thundered at Gráinne the Cook.

'Yes, it is, but the master is out hunting the boar in yonder woods and he is definitely not likely to be home before Sunday.'

'Never mind, I'll be pleased to wait for him,' laughed the knight. 'Particularly as I believe it will be no boring proposition with all these flitches of bacon, smoked joints, and delicious looking cheeses hanging down from the ceiling wherever you look!' He gave such a mighty laugh that the pans dropped from their hooks on the walls.

'I am surprised at Finn having made do with only one door in this castle though,' he said, trying to find out if the castle had some secret opening through which one might invade it.

For it was none other than himself who was under orders from his King to land with his troops near Ventry while Finn would be fighting the monster!

'One door is good enough for Finn. For him, his men and myself, and it was obviously good enough for you as well,' answered Gráinne confidently. 'Why should Finn's castle need more than one door?'

The knight mused for a while trying to think of what to say in reply. At this moment the sky just happened to become overcast and a heavy rain began to fall and the Big Man said, 'What do they do when there is a great wind and a downpour or hail blowing in so that the door won't open and nobody is able to get in and out? This is no pleasure for Finn and his men when they are in a hurry to reach home and to find a refuge from the stormy weather in his strong castle and have no door on the sheltered side!'

'Oh,' rejoined Gráinne without a moment's hesitation. 'When something of the kind happens they just catch the castle in their arms and twist it round so that the door is always on the sheltered side; as simple as that!'

'They must be very strong men,' the knight stuttered. 'Tell me how they have come to possess such strength?'

At that moment Finn turned over in the box till it bounced on the floor. It seemed to him that the Big Man had been asking far too many questions.

'What's that?' the knight exclaimed seizing the handle of his twelve-feet-long sword. 'The flour-box prances like a stallion; this is too much to endure!'

'That's no flour-box; it is a cradle of the kind we make here for babies,' said Gráinne like a proud mother, and the knight immediately paced up to the box to have a closer look.

'Such a big baby?' he was struck by Finn in his blanket from which only his head stuck out. 'What age is the child?'

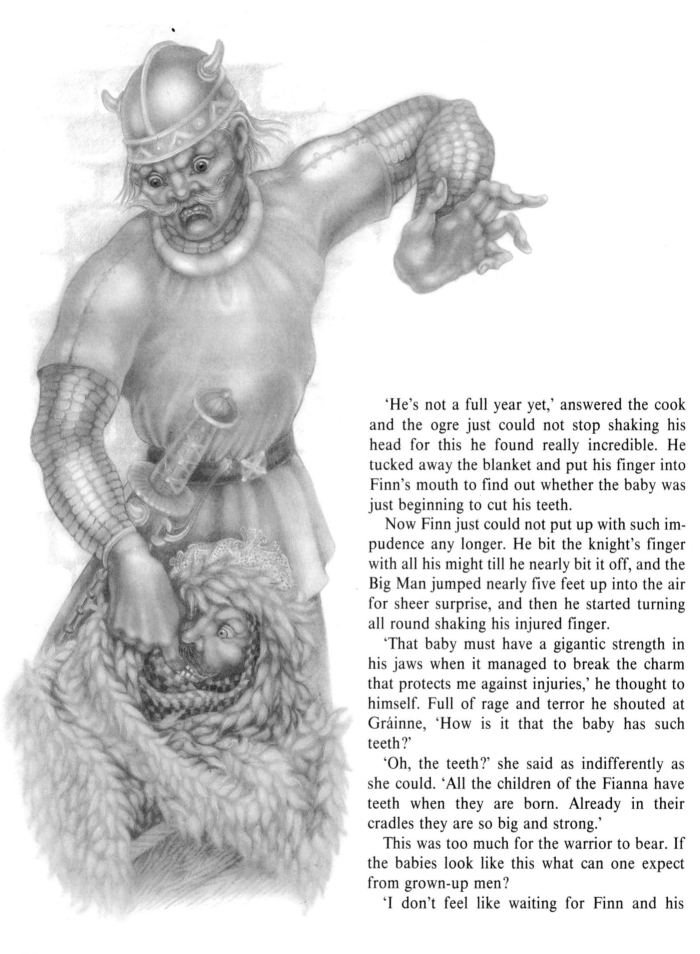

'He's not a full year yet,' answered the cook and the ogre just could not stop shaking his head for this he found really incredible. He tucked away the blanket and put his finger into Finn's mouth to find out whether the baby was just beginning to cut his teeth.

Now Finn just could not put up with such impudence any longer. He bit the knight's finger with all his might till he nearly bit it off, and the Big Man jumped nearly five feet up into the air for sheer surprise, and then he started turning all round shaking his injured finger.

'That baby must have a gigantic strength in his jaws when it managed to break the charm that protects me against injuries,' he thought to himself. Full of rage and terror he shouted at Gráinne, 'How is it that the baby has such teeth?'

'Oh, the teeth?' she said as indifferently as she could. 'All the children of the Fianna have teeth when they are born. Already in their cradles they are so big and strong.'

This was too much for the warrior to bear. If the babies look like this what can one expect from grown-up men?

'I don't feel like waiting for Finn and his

men,' he said to the Cook. 'But we are sure to meet one day anyway,' and he stalked away with long steps the way he had come: from the kitchen into the hall and from the hall out through the door and down hill to the strand where his skiff was waiting.

'I shall have to set out to conquer Finn with a really big army,' he mumbled as he hurriedly set sail for the country where the legendary lake monster lived.

This fearsome monster was all that Finn could think about.

'The soothsayer prophesied that I was to bring this monster to his senses and as such I have no choice,' he said to Gráinne after praising her for having been so clever in showing the giant the door.

He changed the woman's nightcap on his head for a well-burnished helmet, took his sword off the wall, whistled for his young dog Bran and in a moment both of them were running down into the harbour where Finn's slender fighting skiff was at anchor. Finn set sail, and being an expert seaman, reached the country where the lake monster lived long before the warrior did.

Bran the dog caught the scent of the monster from afar and baying wildly, led his master all the way to the lake. High above the surface rose the monster's egg-shaped head on a neck so long that Finn and Bran first thought that they had come upon an enormous snake. There were eight green eyes flashing from the monster's forehead; he used six of them to search the hor-

izon and look out whether men were already bringing him the King's daughter, and with the remaining two he gazed at Finn and his dog.

When the intrepid Bran was about to jump into the water in order to plunge his teeth into the long neck, the monster's cleft tongue flew out of his mouth like a fiery whip. It had nearly coiled round Bran's neck before Finn cut it through with his sword. At that moment the monster blew a blast from his nostrils and began stepping out of the lake on to the shore. It took him a long time to emerge completely, for his body was as gigantic as that of ten whales. The earth trembled under the blows of his tail which he beat wildly against the shore of the lake, and Finn realizing that the monster was challenging him to a duel tightened his grip on his sword.

How small he was with his weapon compared with that mountain of flesh! Indeed, he did not dare to think of the outcome of this struggle, but the oracle which had singled him out for victory had also endowed him with a magic power. He was now able to examine the monster's body through and through as if it had been woven out of a mist — and so he noticed even his black throbbing heart. It did not have its refuge in the breast or anywhere else inside the body as is usually the case with living creatures, but was hidden under one of the monster's six legs where no one would have dreamed of looking for it.

Before the monster managed to swish his fiery tongue against Finn, he jumped near to that spot and buried his sword in the monster up to its hilt. Deprived of strength the monster slipped back into the lake and the surface closed over his body forever.

What was there for them in a foreign land when Ireland, Finn's green mother country, was waiting beyond the sea? So Finn and Bran went back to the skiff and set course for home, but a gale rose suddenly on the high seas driving them back to the shore. The skiff found itself on the pebbles of the strand directly beneath some ugly black stronghold.

'We shall try to hide there before the storm passes, Bran,' said Finn to his dog as he banged at the door.

What a surprise awaited them when the door was opened by a woman almost as big as the warrior from the skiff with the purple sail! She was, in fact, the Big Man's wife, and Finn learned from her that this was his home but its master was not there. She said he had sailed out that very morning with his three sons and the King's troops to Ireland to capture Finn's castle and win the whole of the Irish land for his master.

'A truly royal reward for having freed the King's daughter from her bridegroom of the lake,' thought Finn to himself. But he showed not a sign of any emotion when the warrior's wife was in sight.

'I hear Finn's men can fight like lions. Do you think that your husband is going to beat them?'

'I believe he's going to overwhelm them,' said the warrior's wife proudly. 'My husband is protected by powerful magic against all pains and blows and the irresistible strength of my three sons is held by those three helmets on the wall over there. Until a stranger's hand gets hold of those helmets my sons can fight even the powers of hell.'

Just at that moment a quarrel arose among

the servants, and the warrior's wife ran out to settle it. Finn and Bran remained in the hall all by themselves. The row in the courtyard had no end, and believe it or not, the lady of the house became caught up in it. Finn and his dog ran out unnoticed and disappeared through the gate and behind the first sand dune. They carried with them the three magic helmets.

They were lucky to reach their skiff, and the storm having meanwhile been succeeded by a favourable wind, they soon found themselves on the open sea. They were rapidly approaching the Irish shore. Before they sighted Finn's castle in the distance there were flocks of seagulls circling the masts of the skiff.

'The birds seem to be making strange cries and to have ventured a long way out to sea,' Finn thought to himself. A moment later it became clear why they were doing so.

The birds had been driven away by the din of the battle which was raging right below Finn's castle. Finn's orphaned men were struggling against heavy odds with the attackers who had landed on the shore that morning. It was the knight with his three sons at the head of a mighty host. His invisible magic armour resisted all the blows of the defenders and the knight's three sons were dealing blow after blow with unrelenting strength.

'Hold out, my faithful men!' Finn gave a loud shout with a voice of thunder. The moment the skiff's prow touched the strand, he jumped on to the shore and made his way through the thick of the battle until he came upon the Big Man's three sons.

'Look here, your strength is here in my hands!' he cried lifting the booty from the Big Man's house high over his head: three magic helmets which flashed dazzlingly in the glow of the midday sun. At that moment all the Big Man's three sons dropped their blood-stained swords and sank to their knees like cut-down trees. In the end they rose only to make good their retreat back to their skiffs. In this way they

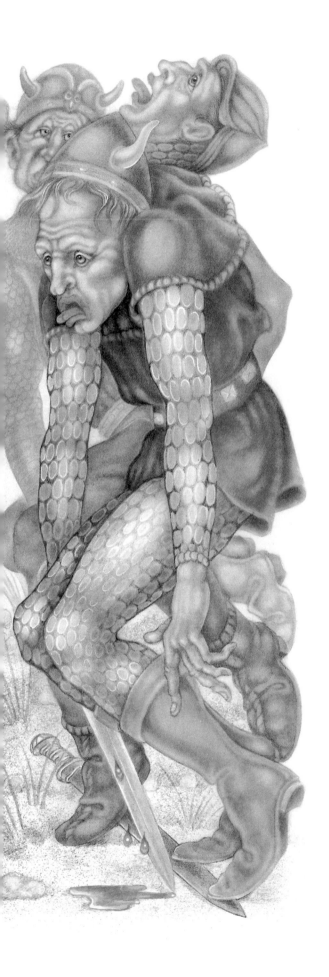

were joined even by their father, the knight, who, having become aware of the real strength of Finn and his men, had lost his previous determination to carry on the fight against them.

'Hurrah!' shouted the defenders and headed by Finn turned the retreat of the enemy troops into a headlong flight. The intruders, confused and horror-stricken, counted themselves lucky in jumping into their skiffs and putting out to the open sea.

'Be grateful that on your home voyage you have your head on your shoulders. Next time you might fare even worse!' shouted Finn after the Big Man by way of farewell. It was indeed the last farewell: for since that day the big warrior never appeared anywhere near Finn's castle again.

Anush Castle
and Its Unfortunate Artificer

Not far from the path leading from ancient Armenia to the city of Ecbatana a steep tower of a rock rose into the sky. Never a handful of soil stuck to it, not a single leaf of grass ever freshened the hard rocky terrain. Only the sun's heat burned it day after day just like in a potter's kiln.

Various pilgrims passed by, and one day it was Farhad the sculptor who wandered into these parts. Though young, his art had already made him famous all over the land. He walked carrying a hammer on his shoulder, head bent and deep in thought; there is always something to brood over for a man who breathes life into stone.

It was only the fanfares of hunting horns which made him raise his head just in time: a pack of greyhounds with whippers-in and falconers nearly dashed him to the ground. The next moment a merry group of hunters galloped along the path amidst a storm of shouts and laughter, and just as quickly disappeared from view.

Farhad was as a man thunderstruck. It was not merely the shock of nearly being knocked over, it was the face of the lady riding with the troupe. She was possessed of a kind of beauty he had never seen before. In that very brief moment the maiden's image became engraved on his heart so deeply that he would never again forget her.

Day after day the sculptor would come back to the steep rock in the hope of seeing the maiden once more, but the merry company of hunters with the fair horsewoman never passed by again.

Many of those who knew Farhad now did not know what to think of him. He seemed to have entirely forgotten his art; all he did was to wander about in the mountains alone as his mind had grown feeble.

Days grew into weeks. Whole months dragged on in his never-ending rambling which always ended in the same place: underneath the steep rock. At last the day came when he did see his fair lady once again, without whippers-in and falconers, on a merry outing accompanied by her suite, she seemed even more charming than the first time. She looked at Farhad and than spurred her horse on to the boulder upon which he was sitting.

'What mystery do these mountains hold for you, master sculptor?' she asked. 'What drives you to wander about in this waste land? I have seen you here a number of times.'

'It was the hope that I might see you again that turned this arid desert into a garden of Eden,' answered Farhad.

'Are you really so much in love?' laughed the maiden.

'Do you think that the heart of a man accustomed to wielding a hammer and chisel had become so hard that there was no room left in it for true beauty?'

'Oh, that is not at all what I think,' said the maiden. 'Why should he who must conquer beauty out of the stone not love that which is beautiful of itself? But now listen carefully, Farhad the sculptor: to win the heart of the daughter of the King of the Arians — for I am she, Princess Anush — demands great sacrifices!'

'I know, great gods and lovely goddesses have a right to demand anything.'

'I will not ask the impossible, Farhad. I only wish to test how much you love me. Do you see the rock over you? It's enough for you to let your eyes wander off me for a while,' and the maiden pointed to the spired top. 'Cut out a castle for me over there. I would like to have a view from its height as far as the Assyrian lowlands and see the silver waters of the Tigris meander in the green leas. I would also wish to catch sight of the slender palm-trees of Bagistana swinging their wide tops in the breeze which blows from the mountains. Also, in the very heart of the rock, I desire to have a treasury for my jewels, and under the walls of the palaces I wish to have stables for my full-blooded horses. When you have finished all this then I shall become your wife.'

Having said this, the daughter of the King of the Arians turned the black horse on his hind legs by a single thrust of rein, and rode down to

join her entourage. In a few moments the whole company had disappeared in clouds of dust raised from the road by the hoofs of the cantering horses.

Farhad remained all alone with his rock. He set the chisel and the first blow of the hammer rang out, and from that moment, day in day out, one blow after the other echoed through the mountains; the love for fair Anush poured iron into Farhad's muscles. Gradually the top of the rock was turning into cosy chambers, noble corridors and magnificently decked halls. Like a miracle, a work of heavenly beauty grew out of the rock. The walls of the palace were enlivened by stone engravings. On them ancient heroes were fighting devils and evil spirits, and the ancient Persian kings won glorious victories over their enemies. However, the sculptor also decorated the castle with glorious deeds of generosity which as the legends told, the rulers of the Arians had performed throughout the land. Let the beloved Anush take pleasure in the nobility of ancestors, herself even more noble than they had been!

At long last Farhad was able to send word to the Princess and announce that the work was done. Anush came accompanied by a bevy of her companions.

'It is indeed pretty,' she said having examined the castle from the underground stables up to the gallery that floated like a little cloud at the point of the highest tower. 'But there is no water here — and I don't see any trees! Make some fountains as well and let the water sprout high through silver veils. Pray, plant some green shrubberies and flowers and trees on the rock so that I can dwell in their shade — and in your arms, Master Sculptor!'

Whereupon the daughter of the King of the Arians whipped her full-blooded steed and cantered off at the head of her suite. Once again Farhad was left alone. He looked round in despair: there was not a single stream in sight, not a single spring from anywhere.

carried fertile soil and distributed it over the terraces. The sprinklers watered the soil and the Master was able to sow the first seeds and to plant the first tree.

Years passed, the trees grew up into shadowy crowns and yielded their first fruits. The platforms on the terraces became covered with carpets of flowers, and nightingales sang in the fragrance of the silvery nights.

Everyone who travelled on the Ecbatana road just had to stand in dumb amazement, for it appeared that the overhanging gardens and the castle above them were floating in the air. However, the one to whom this marvel of marvels was to belong never rode past even once. Day after day Farhad looked out like a beggar for her to come by. He sent one message after another through passers-by, but all in vain.

Then one day when the sun like so many times before bent down above the mountain ranges, he heard a peasant singing a jubilating song. Strangely enough, the man was carrying a big bag on his back and groaning under it. He sat down next to Farhad, for indeed he was in need of a rest. He was wiping streams of sweat from his forehead, yet he did so with a smile on his face.

'Where are you coming from?' asked the sculptor. 'What a happy man you must be when you are singing out so merrily.'

'I am come from the royal city, and why shouldn't I be singing when the whole country is ringing with merrymaking?'

Farhad asked what event people were celebrating. The wayfarer looked at him as if he did not believe his ears.

'Where have you been spending your days if you don't know about our ruler's wedding? It has been on for seven days and nights now. Wine is pouring in streams from the fountains and mountains of savouries are piling up on tables in the open air. Anyone who comes along may eat and drink his fill, and make merry and sing as well, my master. The whole city is strum-

The sculptor became a digger. He dug new beds for distant little streams so as to turn their flow towards the rock topped by the castle. Inside the rock itself he sank corridors to make the water rise through the inside of the mountain up to the castle and complete the work that he had made up his mind to accomplish. First, he carved staircases and terraces into the hillside and built water containers with gargoyles and fountains. From distant slopes he then

ming at the strings and the dancers' feet never get tired. I, too, came into my own and here in my bag I am carrying a parting gift that will see me and my family through for quite a few days.'

'That must truly be a glorious wedding feast,' said Farhad. 'And which beauty is the ruler taking to wife?'

'The only daughter of the King of the Arians, sir. Her name is Anush.'

Hearing these words, Farhad turned deathly pale and became transfixed as though bitten by a cobra. Then without a word he rose and with a sleep-walker's step walked up to the castle. He paced from one terrace to another through the glory of the gardens as far as the main entrance.

There was no lion's head baring its teeth the way it does at other castles. Nor were there any wings of a bird of prey stretching anywhere; in the arch was a likeness of Princess Anush fondling a gentle white dove in the palms of her hands. It was the gentleness and the happiness of love that the castle carved out of the rock was destined to serve, not the cruelties of battles and wars.

Behind the palaces of the second court stood Farhad's workshop. He entered it. There in a row lay the hammers, chisels, picks and cutters as he had arranged them when his work was done. Now he picked up the tools one after another, stroked each of them in turn with his palms, and laid them back again in their places. They had been his friends for a long number of years, none of them had betrayed him.

The heaviest hammer, the one with which he had sunk the chambers for the treasuries, lay at the end of the row. He took it up once again and came out of the workshop in the spot where the rock jutted out into a narrow promontory. From there one had a magnificent view: mountain ranges covered in everlasting snow, rivers flowing through palm groves in the wide open spaces of distant vast plains, and far below the land where the master had worked in days gone by.

He looked around for the last time, and then flung the hammer high up above his head. It rose, turning in the air like a bird shot in the middle of its flight, and a moment later it came down right upon his head.

The craftsman was dead, but in spite of that they called his work by the name of the woman who had betrayed his heart. They began to call it Anush, which means 'the Sweet One'.

The castle had been magically worked out of the rock for human happiness. However, it turned into a palace of tears and suffering, for the Persian rulers made Anush Castle into a prison for the Kings of Armenia who became their captives.

The Villainous Egil

It happened in Denmark during the reign of Canute the Sixth, later to be named Saint Canute, that in the island of Bornholm the administrator of royal property and the King's vice-regent died. It was that very time that a man named Egil, whose father, a true knight who had distinguished himself in the past at the royal court through courage and loyalty, reported for duty to the King.

King Canute received the knight's son with kindness. 'The administrator of my estates on Bornholm has just died. You, Egil, may, if you wish, succeed him. You will test your luck and I will test your loyalty.'

'You know yourself, Your Majesty, that I come of a good family. I will do my best to serve you to your satisfaction,' answered Egil in a voice which smacked of complacency, and that very week he set off for Bornholm. As a well-tried warrior he was not given to procrastination.

Before long those who sailed from time to time between the island and the Danish mainland had quite a few things to report: they said Egil conducted himself on Bornholm like a true vice-regent. He had gathered around him a retinue of the most warlike fellows from the whole island and now kept them most well provided for at his residence. Apart from that, the stronghold was said to be looking more like a castle the way he was building it.

King Canute listened to these reports in silence. At the same time, however, he thought of the new Bornholm administrator with ever-growing mistrust. 'Egil seems to be living beyond his means. His predecessor had conducted himself with much greater modesty. After all, the rocky Bornholm was never too fertile nor too full of cattle, and the people there were not used to seeing even their lords conduct themselves wastefully.'

While King Canute was troubled with such

thoughts, Egil was revelling on Bornholm at the head of his men, day after day and night after night.

When spring was approaching and supplies were running short, the whole host of ruffians and profligates embarked on oar-driven ships with dragon's heads on their prow, and set out across the Baltic Sea into Pomerania against the Slavonic Wends. Give the devil his due: Egil's mercenaries knew equally well how to fight as how to spend their days in feasting. They attacked the fully loaded Wendic merchant ships whilst still on the open sea. They killed off their crews and brought the whole cargo home as loot.

Once again the feasting went on unceasingly and became even noisier than before: the ransacking of the Wendic ships was being celebrated like a naval victory over the enemy. Egil was proud of the way he managed all things, and before long he sent a messenger to the King with the invitation: 'Do me the honour, Canute, and come to visit me on Bornholm. You shall see with your own eyes how well I am doing in my service to you.'

The King accepted the invitation — but what was his surprise when his fleet had anchored near the island and the ruler with his suite disembarked at the Bornholm beach. What he saw on his way to Egil's seat instead of fertile fields was nothing but uncultivated fallow land overgrown with weeds.

However, the stronghold which Canute had last visited while his former administrator was alive, was changed beyond recognition. It was decked with a tower built of mighty logs and a new banqueting hall. The gate was strengthened on both sides with turrets joined together by a covered gallery. Banners flew from it and men in resplendent helmets blew with all their might into oxhorns in honour of the ruler's arrival.

An even more magnificent reception was awaiting the guests in the banqueting hall. The ruler was overwhelmed by the riches and the splendour of the spacious hall. The walls were hung with a great variety of weaponry and covered with rows of battle shields dazzling with the glitter of their mounting and lids. The tables were loaded with dainties such as the ruler himself was unable to afford, and foreign-looking goblets were filled with fragrant mead.

Canute tasted this and that, took a mighty draught from his pitcher and said, 'Excellent mead indeed, but it has a different smell from our own, and from where did smoked meat of boars appear on Bornholm?'

'From as far as the Wends, Your Majesty,' laughed Egil wiping his beard. 'Haven't we got a right to war spoils?'

'Spoils are spoils and plunder is plunder,' answered Canute. 'Since when do the King of Denmark's warriors steal pots and pans from women in kitchens, and smoked meat, flour and honey from their larders? If the fields on Bornholm were duly sown and the cattle properly fed, you would not have to heap dishonour on yourselves nor on myself by acting as robbers of other people's victuals!'

Hearing this, Egil turned pale with rage, frowned like a dozen devils, and clenched his fists under the table. However, he did not say a word in response to the ruler's reproof. After a while, the King's face took on a more benign look and the banquet continued in good spirits, and so it remained during the rest of the time the King dwelt on the island.

Three days later, before embarking on his return voyage, he said goodbye to Egil in a magnanimous mood, but before entering the ship he took the vice-regent aside and reminded him resolutely, 'Remember that I have ordered all those who enjoy the dignity of serving the King to be on their guard on their expeditions by land and sea not to turn into robbers and villains. This is my will and it still applies.'

However, Egil turned his gaze aside, and once again did not say a word in reply. How-

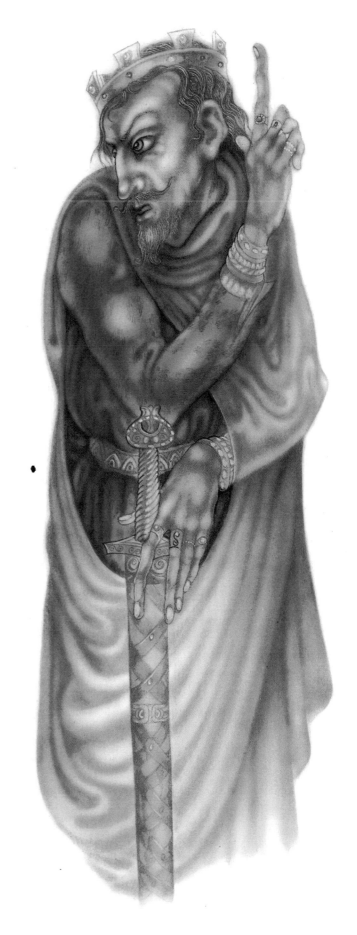

ever, no sooner had the first favourable wind blown over the Baltic than he sailed again to Pomerania and robbed the Wends of as much bounty as the skiffs would hold, for the storehouses on Bornholm were completely empty again and Canute's decree seemed to have sailed away with the King over the boundless waves of the sea.

Having returned from his expedition, Egil issued an order that no one should reveal anything to any stranger. Human beings are talkative creatures however, and this trait is stronger than any injunction. Some time after the administrator's new expedition King Canute did come to learn about it. He made a firm resolution to divest Egil of the office with which he had been entrusted. 'As soon as I find a man to replace him who would be at least half as honest as the administrator before Egil used to be!'

It just so happened at that very time that between Bornholm and the strait of Öresund a big merchant vessel disappeared without leaving any trace behind it. It belonged to rich Norwegian merchants and was loaded to the brim with all kinds of cargoes. Olaf, the King of Norway, himself began to show interest in the mysterious disappearance — indeed, the ship's owners were among the most respected men in the realm and had not been loath to granting loans into the royal exchequer. Before anything else he sent a message to the Danish King Canute, who was his brother-in-law. After all, the ship had sailed in Danish waters and it was not possible that she should have been shipwrecked, indeed, the sea had been calm for many days.

Canute determined to search for the craft himself. The fastest warships were made ready to set sail with a great host of warriors headed by Canute and his brother Benedict. The expedition set off for Bornholm, for it was there the ship was sighted last. When the fleet reached the spot where the high Bornholm shore came within view several smaller islands appeared. These were nothing but stones and cliff, but

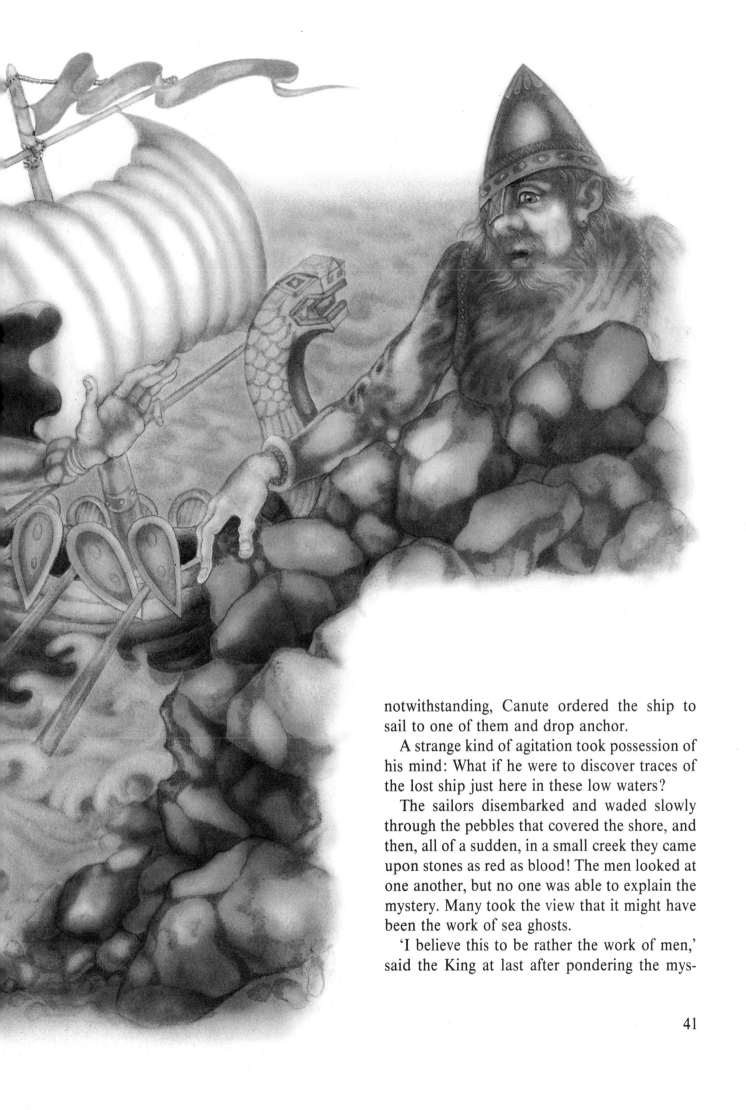

notwithstanding, Canute ordered the ship to sail to one of them and drop anchor.

A strange kind of agitation took possession of his mind: What if he were to discover traces of the lost ship just here in these low waters?

The sailors disembarked and waded slowly through the pebbles that covered the shore, and then, all of a sudden, in a small creek they came upon stones as red as blood! The men looked at one another, but no one was able to explain the mystery. Many took the view that it might have been the work of sea ghosts.

'I believe this to be rather the work of men,' said the King at last after pondering the mystery, then gave the resolute order: 'To Bornholm!'

'If what I believe to have happened is indeed the truth, then the mysterious disappearance of the Norwegian ship will be solved,' he said to himself.

They did not reach Bornholm before darkness had fallen, and, acting on the King's order, disembarked in utter silence. They would not have been sighted from Egil's seat even in daytime for there was a high rock towering up between the castle stronghold and the place of landing. The armed men headed by the King took quarters in the nearest royal estate.

The ruler called aside his brother and two well-tried commanders, Svend and Astrid, for taking counsel. 'There can be no more opportune moment than the present,' whispered Canute. 'Can you hear the din of drinking songs coming from the stronghold all the way down here? Egil is having a feast with his men as usual. Take a company of the most experienced warriors and bring the administrator here to this very table for trial!'

Obeying the King's orders, the commanders brought their armed men through the gate past the drunken guards, and quickly surrounded Egil's timber banqueting chalet. Svend and Astrid remained with the men, and Benedict went inside. 'King Canute is calling you, Egil!' he shouted on the threshold. 'He wishes to ask you what you know of the vanished Norwegian ship!'

If at that moment a turbulent sea had flooded the hall, Egil could not have been more astounded. He jumped up from his seat like a wild beast with his sword drawn and shouted to his guests, 'To arms!'

At that moment the shutters flew apart with a clink, and the spears, axes and hammers of

Canute's men appeared in the windows. The torchflames were set in motion by a sudden draught, making the soldiers' helmets glisten above their determined faces.

'You would be better advised, Egil, to order your men to lay down their arms in peace,' Benedict continued as though nothing had happened. 'Let's go to face the King!'

Seeing that it would indeed be foolish to test their swords against such odds, Egil surrendered to Benedict, who straight away brought him before the King. Meanwhile Svend and Astrid stayed in the castle with their warriors to prevent any of Egil's boon companions from escaping.

'We have not seen each other for a long time now, Egil,' said the King to his administrator. 'Nevertheless, I would not mind if our meeting today were to be our last.'

'That depends entirely upon your own will, Sir,' rejoined Egil. 'But I hope you don't think that someone will regard you as a better ruler for having your faithful servants arrested for enemies.'

'The enemies of King Olaf who burn Norwegian ships are also my enemies, Egil!' thundered Canute. Everything had depended on this moment. Indeed, when he had discovered strange red stones before Bornholm, it occurred to him that intense heat might have been the cause. What else could have caused such a burning heat on a hollow piece of land than

the fire of a big wooden ship? Who else but the experienced raider Egil could have set fire to such a vessel in those places?

'I have no other evidence against Egil than his own bad conscience. If I suddenly accuse him of this villainous act, and if he really did commit the crime, his look and conduct will give him away!' This was what the King had mused upon during his voyage from the little island to Bornholm, and now it turned out that his guess had been right. Hearing the King's words, Egil remained as if thunderstruck. He had not an inkling of the red stones left behind by the huge fire. He had sailed off with the spoils long before the Norwegian ship burnt out, firmly convinced that the waves of the tide would wash away the remains long before another day had dawned. Now flabbergasted by the truthful indictment he lost his head completely. He fell to his knees, and told the King the whole story.

King Canute listened with his eyes turned to the ground, and a long silence ensued before he uttered the words of his sentence.

'I can see, Egil,' he said, 'that you have truly tested your luck. Not as an administrator faithful to my royal will, but as a self-styled robber who, not satisfied with that, felt compelled to turn to piracy. You have chosen your own path, now all that is left to you is to choose the tree on which the hangman shall hang you. You must know the punishment for such crimes.'

The sentence was carried out that very day in the nearby forest, and immediately afterwards Canute entered the stronghold with his army to pass sentences upon Egil's companions. No one went unpunished, and as the old chronicles tell he destroyed the den of thieves on Bornholm once and for all.

44

How Wartburg Castle Came to Be Built

The castle of Wartburg has been called 'the pearl of Thuringia', because it almost seems to glisten amidst the green hills of the Thuringian Forest like a rare jewel. It was founded by Landgrave Ludwig nine centuries ago and an old legend tells what a clever trick made it possible.

In those days Ludwig was among the foremost noblemen in the region. However, his neighbours, the lords of Frankenstein, did not feel themselves to be any worse than he: their land stretched as far as Eisenach, which meant a great deal in those days.

The Tafelberg Hill, however, was still within the precints of Ludwig's hunting grounds, and it was along its flat top that the lord, in company with his fellow hunters was driving his best steed one day in pursuit of a fine stag. Just at the moment Ludwig raised his spear to fling it, the deer bounded away into the undergrowth. A sixteen-tined stag, such a prize was not one that Ludwig was willing to give up just because of some thicket! He chased the stag as fast as

45

the horse's feet would go, and lo, like a phantom the animal's horns could be seen flashing as far down as the bed of the little stream. However, before the hunter could manage to halt the horse and take a steadier aim, the stag jumped across to the other bank. On and on did the nobleman pursue the velvet horns vanishing and reappearing behind the leafy curtain on the opposite slope. Up and up the slopes he went and down and down to the other side, from hill to hill in a wild chase until the nobleman's hunting party was left heaven knows how far behind, and the stag had also vanished from sight. When Ludwig's foaming horse just about managed to stumble up the next hilltop, all the nobleman could manage to do was to wave his hand in despair and give the chase up as lost.

A moment later, however, all thoughts of the stag flew from his mind, for the view that opened to all quarters from the top of the hill was so splendid that lord Ludwig found himself turning round and round for quite a while not knowing where to direct his gaze first over that lovely Thuringian countryside.

'No, this is a view I am not going to part with easily,' said the noble to himself. 'And I will enjoy it from windows that will be mine; I will build myself a castle on this hill!'

Meanwhile, even his belated hunting party had at last reached the top, headed by the steward of Ludwig's domains, his lord's right hand. This time the lord welcomed him with a truly unexpected order, 'Tomorrow you shall bring here from Eisenach an architect to make measurements for walls, towers, and a palace!'

'But the hill does not come under your domain, Sir. While chasing the stag you have crossed the border of your land. We now find ourselves on grounds of the lords of Frankenstein!'

Ludwig turned pale with anger. The lords of Frankenstein of all people! All the way back to his seat of Schauenburg he thought of nothing else but how to turn the tables on his age old adversaries. As he passed through the gate of the Schauenburg courtyard an excellent idea flashed across his mind. That very day he had six slender firs cut down in the forest and their stems made into two wooden barriers painted over with the colours of his own coat of arms.

The next day before dark a carriage thoroughly greased on pivot and axle left the castle, and wobbled silently into the places where the day before lord Ludwig had chased the sixteen-tined stag. Freshly painted posts and poles jutted out of the wagon and along the sides, seated in their saddles, rode silent servants and an even more taciturn steward. If the latter did not shake his head from time to time like one who had no idea what was occurring, it would have seemed he had fallen asleep in the saddle.

In the dead of night they reached the spot below the hill top upon which their lord had

found himself captivated by the unexpected view. They dumped the load from the waggon, carried it up to the top, put together the painted barriers, and early in the morning turned back, still under cover of darkness. At midday the steward was able to announce at Schauenburg Castle that the barriers stood exactly the way Ludwig had graciously desired them to stand.

'It is not my place, Sir, to question your wishes, but you know just as well as I do that the Frankensteins are not going to allow anyone to occupy a single inch of their land,' the steward reminded him.

Nor was he mistaken; in a few days a messenger from the Frankensteins came galloping to Schauenburg carrying a very angry letter for the lord. It ended in a question, 'What are those railings of yours upon our hill supposed to mean?'

Prince Ludwig pulled up his belt and said: 'Go and tell your masters that I have only righted an old wrong. That hill once belonged to my family and knowledge of this fact was somehow lost with time.'

The lords of Frankenstein took the matter before the court, and the court having heard both contending parties passed the following verdict, 'If twelve virtuous knights swear that the contended piece of land is indeed part of Ludwig's dominion let possession pass once and for all to his hands.'

It was with a sad heart that Ludwig returned from the hearing. He himself knew best that the hill with the beautiful view had never belonged

to his family property and that the stories about a heritage from his ancestors were but his own invention. Twelve knights good and true could certainly be found among his vassals, but a renowned knight cannot perjure himself, by thunder!

'I simply must build a castle upon the hill with the fine view now I have set my mind on it!' cried the nobleman, striking the table with his fist. He tore down a crossbow from the wall and set off down to the pond to hunt wild ducks to take his mind off things.

It was along the brook that the pond was most easily accessible. Its banks were bordered by thick willows, and the lord was at times forced to pass through a curtain of long bendy willow wands. Suddenly a wonderful idea came

into his mind. 'Aren't there enough baskets, wicker-baskets and panniers made of this blessed wood both in the castle and the cottages?'

Ludwig half closed his eyes against the sun like a fox who scents the sweet smell of the prey.

That very day he had it proclaimed that the next day at daybreak all the serfs from the neighbourhood should stand with their teams of oxen and with all their baskets, wicker-baskets and panniers along the moat. It would be necessary to have it deepened and cleared of the drifted soil!

That morning the nobleman personally supervised the work to make sure it would proceed the way he had ordered. All that morning baskets full of soil travelled along the chain of human hands up to be emptied into the waggons and then thrown back into the moat. The moment the waggons were full they set off on Ludwig's orders along the road leading to the wooded hilltops. They followed the same track that the carriage loaded with the barriers had done.

Suddenly Ludwig, leading a troupe of twelve vassals overtook the carriages at a gallop. On a hill in the Thuringian Forest there was a pleasant surprise waiting for the knights, lord Ludwig promised with an enigmatic smile.

The lovely view from the top of the hill was a surprise in itself — even more so were the tables full of food and drink, a magnificent feast under the golden October sun. While the party was feasting to their hearts' content, the serfs were carrying up to the top the first baskets from the carriages which had meanwhile reached the foot of the hill. A brown dam of soil began to pile up.

The enlivened knights, yielding to curiosity rose from the tables, and before long the first of them were scrambling up the dam. 'Is it because the hills of the Frankenstein hunting grounds are so low, Sir, that you wish to push them up higher?'

Ludwig was laughing with the others; indeed, he was no spoilsport. 'Just scramble up, my faithful ones, and have no fear. You are treading on my own land, for haven't the waggons brought the honest soil of Schauenburg up here?'

'It is indeed true, Sir, that we are standing on your land every one of us,' cried the knights who were now laughing their heads off, drawing their swords and sticking them into the mound. 'We can swear to the whole world that our swords stick in your soil up to their hilts!'

Joke or no joke, the oath remained an oath and not one of the knights took it back, even when brought before the Imperial Court.

So the hill with its lovely view became the property of nobleman Ludwig, and the carriages that had brought up the Schauenburg soil were soon to transport building stone as well. Castle walls, the brickwork of buildings, watchtowers as well as the citadel rose up quickly and the castle was named Wartburg.

Ludwig's witty ruse which is said to have made it possible to build the castle in the beautiful location where it stands seems to have settled in its foundations. Instead of the clash of swords and the din of battle, clever songs accompanied by the sweet sound of lutes would echo around the courtyard, and years later, Ludwig's art-loving grandson turned Wartburg into a sanctuary for Germany's best poets and singers.

The Gap of Gobelin

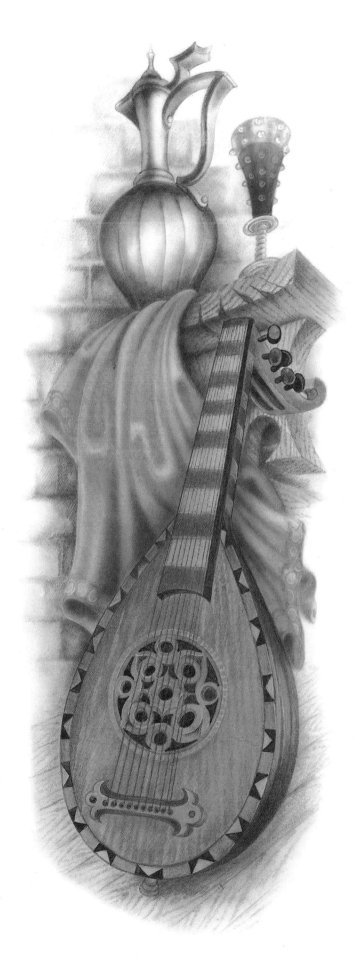

All that is left of the castle of Mortain which used to stand under Normandy Downs are the remains of some vaulted brickwork and a mysterious black hole leading down into the earth. The people in the country call it the Gap of Gobelin, and there is a dark prophecy about it which says that whoever falls down Gobelin's gap shall never return to the earth again.

Once upon a time the castle of Mortain was owned and ruled by Sir Guillaume de Mortain. He had a reputation of extreme cruelty in battle, and this helped him defeat hosts of enemies. It was with equal cruelty that he ruled his dominion. Nothing was allowed to oppose his lust or whims, and there was hardly a serf, or even a squire, far and wide who did not feel de Mortain's contempt on his own skin. Equally cold and indifferent was de Mortain's behaviour towards his own wife. After years of marriage she finally worried herself to death. Lord de Mortain, on the other hand, was constantly in the highest spirits. He twisted his moustaches the way military men were wont to do, and whistled away at military marches which indeed were the only tunes he knew.

Even though his wife had only just died, de Mortain decided to remarry as soon as possible. So he set about riding out to hunt and no longer just for the sake of the hares and the antlered deer. Rather, he would search for high-born brides throughout the neighbourhood. Though he was no beau and his hair was like a tuft of dried up winter grass, hardly anyone was his match in daintiness; not one of the marriageable noble young ladies was to his taste. He crossed and recrossed the whole region, ventur-

51

ing ever farther and farther, until one day he came upon a little village with a modest squire's manor. He tied his horse in front of the gate and went in to ask for a drink of water.

However, when at the squire's call a maiden appeared with a tray and a tin pitcher, he forgot all about thirst and stood like one gazing at a vision. It was no wonder, for the squire's daughter, Iolande, was so lovely that she might easily have been crowned Queen of Beauties for the whole of Normandy.

'I like your daughter very much,' said de Mortain to the squire. 'I will marry Iolande in the church of Mortain before the plums have ripened on the trees.'

Now it was the squire who stood dumbfounded. For he himself, Iolande's father, was younger than this unbidden wooer! For a spell he tried to talk de Mortain out of the idea. His daughter, he argued, was still very young and had no thought of getting married. However, it was hard to argue with a lord whose savagery made everyone in those parts quake at the knees. After all, the squire himself was de Mortain's vassal.

'Do you mean to say you can't give orders to your own daughter?' cried Guillaume de Mortain. 'Enough of idle talk, I am in a hurry. Tomorrow I will send a sedan to fetch your daughter. As to her trousseau and dowry you do not have to worry. Anyway, I can see you are as poor as a church mouse,' he sneered, and instead of saying goodbye, he swung up into the saddle and raised a cloud of dust from under the horse's hoofs right into the squire's face.

When the unfortunate father told his daughter what the lord de Mortain had set his mind on, she turned deathly pale, but then she said with conviction in her heart, 'I will never become the wife of Guillaume de Mortain. Never shall I become his property!'

The squire lowered his face so that she

should not see how red with shame he had turned. He found not a word of response to the maiden's refusal, so ashamed was he of his cowardice, but far greater was his fear of what the next day would bring. However, when de Mortain's servants did really appear the next morning with the sedan, Iolande said goodbye to her father without a word of reproach and without tears.

'She wishes to spare me de Mortain's anger, she loves me more than I thought she did. Why was it just our manor that had to be afflicted with such a misfortune?' said the squire to himself as the sedan disappeared into the distance. As he stood and looked down the road with tears flowing from his eyes he cried: 'Forgive me, my daughter, oh, forgive me!'

Lord Guillaume welcomed Iolande in his seat with wheedling courting. He had had the chambers in the main tower prepared for her and filled with brocade and precious jewels.

'Her feminine desire for fine clothes shall not resist such wedding presents. She shall give in before long, and be glad to become the wife of the greatest lord in these parts,' muttered Guillaume de Mortain under his breath.

Iolande, however, did not even glance at the chests, and the harder the lord of the castle pressed her to grant him his wish, the icier was the face she turned on him.

'All right,' said de Mortain at last when he realized that all his efforts had come short of his expectations. 'I can see you will need some time to come to your senses. Until that happens

the trees. I do not intend to become an idle tattler, my dear! In exactly five days the castle chaplain is going to marry us at the local church.'

The maiden rose from the chair with such defiance and anger in her eyes that lord Guillaume involuntarily started back a step.

'You are paler than a dead man's candle,' he said. 'As from tomorrow you shall be allowed to walk about under the tower as far as the orchard. Before the wedding merrymaking comes along, your cheeks will have turned rosy like the apples on my trees.'

Poor Iolande could scarcely hide her joy; in her eyes a flicker of hope appeared.

De Mortain pretended not to have noticed anything, but he added at once, 'You will not have to fear for your safety in the least, my dear! My seat is walled-in with battlements high enough to prevent any blackguard from getting inside should he happen to think of kidnapping you!'

The next day, when Iolande ran down from the tower, she joyfully breathed in the fresh morning air, listened to the lovely chirping of the birds, and smelled the fragrance of the bright chalices of the flowers. When she reached the orchard, she enjoyed the apples the like of which only the soil of Normandy can produce, and then continued her morning walk.

The castle was truly spacious. After a while she found herself in a remote corner of the fortification where high grass, brushwood and age-old trees had grown together into an impassable wilderness. All of a sudden the rotten branches gave way with a loud crack beneath her foot, which had become stuck in a gap which was overgrown with hair-grass. Having carefully drawn aside some brambles, she noticed two steps ahead of her a vaulted opening into the ground through which she could see a narrow, crumbling staircase which disappeared in the black depths as though leading the way to the very bowels of the Earth. Hesitating, Iolande

you shall remain locked up in the Mortain tower which will be your prison.'

So day after day de Mortain visited the tower, never ceasing to urge the maiden to become his wife, but all to no avail.

De Mortain was not really a man accustomed to long periods of waiting, and one day he announced to Iolande: 'The summer is drawing to its close, and I told your father that we would get married before the plums had ripened on

put her foot on the first step, then on the second, the third, until she found herself in an underground passage.

Icy water dripped from the stone vault there, and a cold musty smell wafted across the maiden's face; should she go on, or turn back? No, she would bravely step out into the unknown even if the road should lead straight to hell!

Iolande picked her way step by step through the impenetrable darkness, and just at the moment when it seemed that the passage would never end, she caught sight of a dim light in the distance. As she stumbled along nearer and nearer to it, it became ever more clear that it was the light of day shining through among the overhanging branches. She had reached her goal — she got to the other end of the passage.

Pushing the branches apart, Iolande saw a grassy clearing in front of her. It opened before her like a soft welcoming palm, but all around, as far as the eye could see, there was a deep blue forest. At the edge of the clearing stood a little cottage with a goat-shed, and a little farther on by the brook she saw a woman doing her washing.

Iolande came running down the slope.

'How do you come to be here, dear girl? How did you manage to get through the woods and marshes?' the old woman wondered. 'Do you know that I hardly meet anyone here all year long?'

So Iolande told her the whole story: about the underground passage, about Guillaume de Mortain, and the reason why she had escaped from him.

The old woman looked into Iolande's eyes. 'I believe you,' she said after a while. 'You may

stay with me and keep house here in my little cottage, and everything is sure to work out all right in the end.'

Meanwhile, the guards at the watch-towers and battlements of Mortain Castle called the alarm: Miss Iolande had not returned from her walk. She had disappeared, she was gone!

Like a mad dog de Mortain began to run about through the courtyards, the garden, the orchard, the high grass, and even along the walls! At last! In a remote corner he spotted the tip of Iolande's veil! De Mortain rushed to a spot where someone had obviously cleared a path for himself. Leaves and branches pushed apart, a dark opening, and on the step the print of a girl's shoe: but this was not the way she could have escaped, the underground passage was blocked. Indeed, even in the time of Guillaume's father the ceiling had caved in!

Notwithstanding, Guillaume de Mortain hurled himself down the steep stairs like one demented.

All night the servants searched by torchlight for the master who failed to return. When at dawn they came upon an uncovered gap, a number of men went down the hole. However, before long they were back: 'There is only some old rubble and rot, no more!'

Since that day the arrogant lord of the castle was never seen again. Years afterwards people christened the ravine the Gap of Gobelin.

As for Iolande, not long after that event she was able to embrace her father again. The old woman had guided her home along a covert path only to vanish back into the forest as though she had never existed.

The Vanished Castle near Koprivnica

To this day a mountain in the vicinity of the Yugoslav town of Koprivnica is called 'The Old Castle', reputedly because it had once been the site of the legendary castle of Prince Marko. This ruler is widely remembered throughout the Balkans. He was a ruler who looked after the welfare of his people, never allowing his subjects to suffer from want, and bravely defending them against the predatory raids of the Turks.

Good friends were what he valued most of all in life, so when one day a messenger reached the castle near Koprivnica with the news that the Turks had put in prison three of his most faithful friends, his eyes flashed with terrible anger.

He ordered the marshal to have Sharac, his favourite steed, harnessed, and then he had the table laid for dinner.

'Why so early tonight, dear husband,' asked Elen, his wife, when they were seated at the table where the Prince's most favourite dish was laid before them: a pile of rice on an enormous silver dish and three apples as big as pumpkins.

'On this very night, Elen, I am going to set out for Varazdin to free my friends from the Turkish jail. They have managed to send a secret letter all the way up to my hands. They will be waiting for me to cut their fetters with my sword.'

Having said this, the Prince fell to his food and put away so much of it that it would do any ordinary mortal for a week. He drank a cask of wine, set a cap of a wolf's fur decked with a silver feather upon his black locks of hair, and took farewell of his wife saying,

'I don't know how long my expedition is going to take — the Turks are holding Varazdin with a force of a mighty host. That's why I hand over the government of the land into your hands, Elen. Be a good manager and ruler, and above all take care that our people should not grow any poorer. Don't impose even a single copper more in taxes on anyone. When I return you shall render me the accounts, remember that!'

The Prince left the castle in good spirits. The town of Varazdin and the whole of its environs was teeming with Turks, and the walls of the Varazdin jail were as thick as those of a fortress; but was not Marko's right hand strong enough and his sword weighty enough, and Sharac, his steed, faithful to the death? It was at that moment that Marko recalled how Sharac had one day, with his own body, saved him from a certain death at the hands of his enemies. His heart was suffused with such feelings of gratitude that in descending the steep mountain paths he jumped off the saddle to take the load off the animal.

In the meadow by the lake Sharac was given the usual draught of wine from the cask as was his wont, neither did his master forget to have a draught himself. Actually, it was not only for the sake of Sharac that Marko halted in that spot: the lake was the home of a water-nymph able to see into the future.

'Come out, dear little sister,' the Prince begged in a whisper. He knew that fairies have soft little ears as if made of silk and cannot bear being addressed aloud. 'Come out of your water realm, and reveal to me when shall I return from this journey?'

A shining little cloud of mist rose and swirled above the lake, and suddenly a goldenhaired maiden stood before the Prince smiling sadly.

'You are destined to fight many skirmishes

and battles, brother, before your friends get out of the jail! It will not be less than three years before the guards on the ramparts of your castle welcome you back with great joy!'

Marko hung his head sadly. At that moment he felt a caress of the fairy's palm softer than the tepid night breeze that rises from the lake in summer. 'You are fond of saying, dear brother, that you have been endowed with a magic power possessed by children and dogs. When these two creatures run, anybody will set upon them apace and pursue them, but lo, when the child or the dog turns round and sallies forth against his pursuers! Then they rapidly beat their retreat no matter how numerous they may be.'

The Prince only smiled, then he jumped into the saddle and rode out to meet both his friends and foes.

In those days the Prince's wife Elen did not enjoy untroubled sleep. For a long time now she had envied her husband his heroic glory, and yearned to surpass him at least in one particular. Would this not be a grand opportunity now that he had departed?

'He prefers to let his serfs and not himself grow rich. The castle treasury is as good as empty, even now.'

She made up her mind that from next day she would increase every serf's tax by one copper. 'I shall see what profit this will bring in.'

As she had resolved, so did she do. Believe it or not, in three years the extra copper amassed

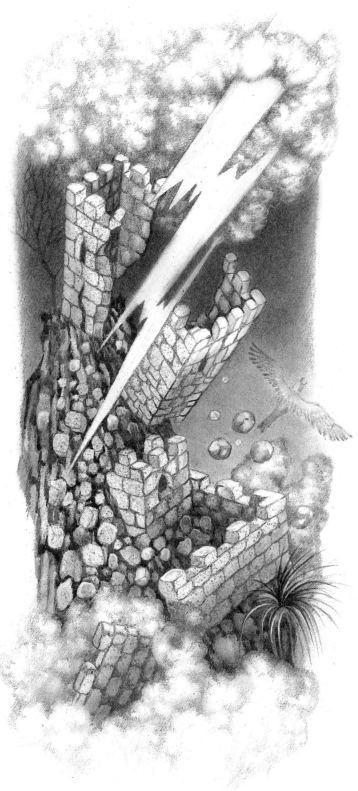

such riches that it overflowed from the coffers and the treasury chamber was filled to the ceiling with piled up coins.

Just as long did it take Marko to free his friends from the jail and at last, after many encounters, he fought his way into his land and to his castle. The water-nymph's prophecy did come true.

'Did you rule your people with justice?' asked the Prince his wife after they had given each other proper welcome. 'Did you manage your land well?'

'Come with me and you shall see with your own eyes,' said Elen instead of replying, and led the Prince into the castle treasury. Marko was rooted to the ground with amazement.

'Long had been your reign in this land, my dear,' said Elen with pride in her voice, 'and in all that time you had not saved up through careful housekeeping even a small part of what I have done in three years. All I did was to raise the serfs' taxes by a mere copper!'

'What do you say?' cried the Prince turning deathly pale. 'You have gone against my wishes, have you? It's out of my people's labour that this property has been squeezed? Cursed be your greed, and you yourself be cursed, wife, and with you the whole of this castle which houses your wicked spoils!'

After these words a roll of thunder boomed out and the sky was filled with a ghastly pale glow. The rock beneath the castle split into two parts forming a great chasm, and the whole structure vanished in the depths of the mountain forever. Only Prince Marko on his faithful steed Sharac lived to ride away from those gruesome horrors and continued to remain a faithful leader to the sorely tried people of the Balkans.

How the Lord of Montferrand Became a Troubadour

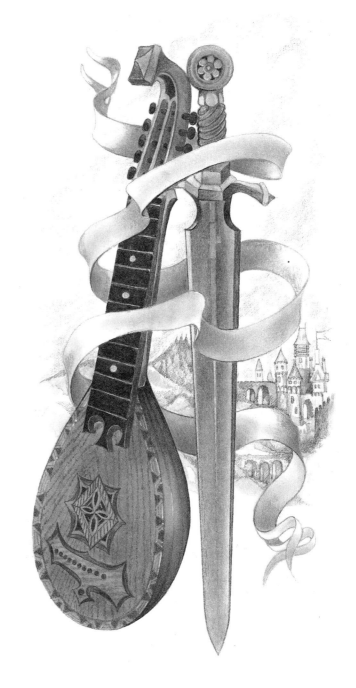

There has never been a shortage of kingdoms in the world. Of course, France could, on top of that, boast a principality called 'le Dauphiné'. It lay in Auvergne which is one of the most beautiful parts of France even to this day. However, it has always been a tough mountainous region and its inhabitants were wont to grapple with poverty which they did with pride and honour.

The story goes that not even the owner and lord of the 'principality', the Dauphin of Auvergne, was exempt from this. 'Dauphin' means 'prince and successor to the throne', but this particular 'successor' was unable to succeed to any throne. Of course, his castle on Montferrand, the memory of which is preserved in the name of the city of Clermont-Ferrand, really looked like a seat of some king, and the landlord behaved accordingly.

He gave magnificent feasts in which the best musicians and jugglers performed, and no sooner had spring arrived than the wide meadow underneath the castle resounded with the clamour of knightly tourneys. The finest lords and ladies from throughout half the country would gather there. Enormous marquees offering refreshments, richly decorated pavilions and palisades shone with bright colours, as did the streamers under the blue skies, and knights on caparisoned steeds were doing their best to throw each other from the saddle with long lances. The Dauphin of Auvergne loved putting on

tourneys and was even numbered among the renowned contestants. However, what he was keenest on was distributing prizes.

'Silver cups? At my tourneys I give these at best to the vanquished as a consolation prize!' he would mock when it sometimes fell to him at a neighbouring castle to be awarded such a prize.

This was not a lie, for at joustings given by himself the victors could look forward to receiving swords of Damascus steel, gold-inlaid harness, girdles set with precious stones. Indeed,

the lord of Montferrand would drive as far as Genoa in Italy and pay piles of gold coins to buy them.

Though the tourneys cost the lord Dauphin of Auvergne even more than the feasts, they were far from being the most expensive of his pleasures. 'I would part with my last shirt,' he would say in jest over a cup of wine, 'for a good troubadour.'

Indeed, the castle teemed with poets and singers, who were not only good but jolly company as well, and there was hardly a more grateful listener than the Dauphin of Auvergne. Nor was there a more generous host to exceed him for these fellows were at liberty to dwell at Montferrand at their pleasure. They drank and sang until the flames of candles in the chandeliers jumped up and down, and when at last they said goodbye one fine day, they carried away purses stuffed with gold coins as a reward for their art.

What wonder then that the lord Dauphin's treasuries were becoming more and more depleted? However, the Dauphin did not worry unduly about that. There was always someone willing to lend money to the owner of such an imposing castle. So the debts grew until lord Dauphin himself no longer knew how much they actually amounted to altogether. The debtors however, had everything counted up to the last penny.

One day it came to light that the Dauphin's debt amounted exactly to the worth of all his forests, fields, meadows, villages and estates of the whole of his domain. Unless the good Dauphin wished to go to jail, all that was left to him was to settle his debts by selling his own property.

All that remained to him now was his castle, but there were no longer sounds of merry-making to be heard from the banqueting hall. Now that the lord was able to offer nothing but a modest peasant fare and a pitcher of water, his noble neighbours began to give a wide berth to Montferrand Castle. A bitter silence settled inside the bare walls, and the courtyard gate remained locked and bolted. The Dauphin of Auvergne became a recluse.

Only Martial, his castellan, remained faithful to his master as before, and patiently listened to his lamentations.

'A friend in need is a friend indeed; beyond all treasures of the world do I now value this proverb,' mused the lord of the castle in his mirthless mood. 'Only at this moment have I come to realize, Martial, that it is just you who are a true friend of mine.'

'There is another proverb, sir, which says: It's no use crying over spilt milk!' rejoined Martial. 'Pull yourself together, and show your false

friends that there is no misfortune that can break the Dauphin of Auvergne. Go on fighting them at tourneys. Indeed, the ransom of the defeated is often not to be spurned.'

'The ransom?' repeated the lord of the castle musingly. 'Ransom for victory!' he shouted delightedly now and embraced the castellan for sheer joy. 'Thanks for the advice, Martial, many thanks! It has just occurred to me how I am going to win back my lost domain!'

The dark thoughts vanished from Montferrand Castle with the wind. All that resounded in the courtyard now day after day were the blows dealt by the Dauphin's powerful arm to the stuffed leather bag which leant against the wall of the rampart. It was the lord of Montferrand

busy training the turns and feints of the jousting art.

Now that the Dauphin no longer gave tourneys, there were others who did, and these jousts were the talk of the whole neighbourhood. One victory after the other was gained by a knight with a covered face. Unlike the others he was not fighting for a prize of honour or for ladies' admiration. When he unhorsed his opponent he pointed the edge of his sword against his throat. According to an old tourney rule the victor had a right to the loser's life, and the defeated man was left with no other choice than to ransom himself with a properly rounded pouch of gold coins rather than let himself be run through with the sword.

Thus did the unknown knight carry off the prize of victory at all tourneys and jousts which were no longer thought to be worth attending unless he was present.

The day came when the unknown knight succeeded in unsaddling the richest nobleman in the whole country. The ransom was raised accordingly for the defeated man ransomed his life with an amount three times higher than usual. The mysterious victor no longer contained himself. He took down his helmet and proudly called to the grandstands, 'Today I have gained the whole town of Clermont together with its neighbourhood by my victory in the fight!' The amazed spectators rose from their benches: the unknown knight was their neighbour the Dauphin of Auvergne!

Yes, it was true: the Dauphin of Auvergne had been winning back his lost estate by his victories. From the ransom gained, he redeemed the forest, the manor, the chalet with the sheep, the manorial mill and by the prize he won that very day regained even the last part of his property.

His noble neighbours were not niggardly of praise, and began to send letters and messages to Montferrand, 'Should not the lord Dauphin celebrate the regaining of his estates with

a friendly banquet with them, his old friends? They were all eagerly looking forward to his invitation.'

However, the Dauphin of Auvergne did not send a word in reply. He would spend whole long evenings in talking to his faithful Martial, and more and more often he would reach for his lute which hung on the wall behind his head. He went through the strings with his fingertips, and before long the first song echoed under the vault of the banqueting hall.

Until late into the night the lord of the castle and his castellan would sing until one day the news spread that all of a sudden the lord Dauphin had disappeared from his seat altogether. His castellan Martial would have been able to give something away as to his master's whereabouts — but he did not disclose anything no matter how eagerly his noble neighbours questioned him.

However, truth will out. One day a vagrant student, a beggar, of whom there were quite a few wandering about France in those days, brought a great news. In the region of Tourain there was a new troubadour travelling round the castles who was more talented than even the most famous singers-composers from all over France, that is the kind of man he was! Anyway, he seemed to know many of the lords as though they were old friends, though descended from the blood of the successors to the throne; a marvellous thing to hear!

'The Dauphin of Auvergne, who else could it be?' the tale went from ear to ear, and it was no lie.

Thus it was that the Dauphin of Auvergne became a legend, as a man who decided that rather than to feast at his own castle in the embrace of false friends it was more enjoyable to wander about other people's castles as a troubadour.

The Arab
Astrologer

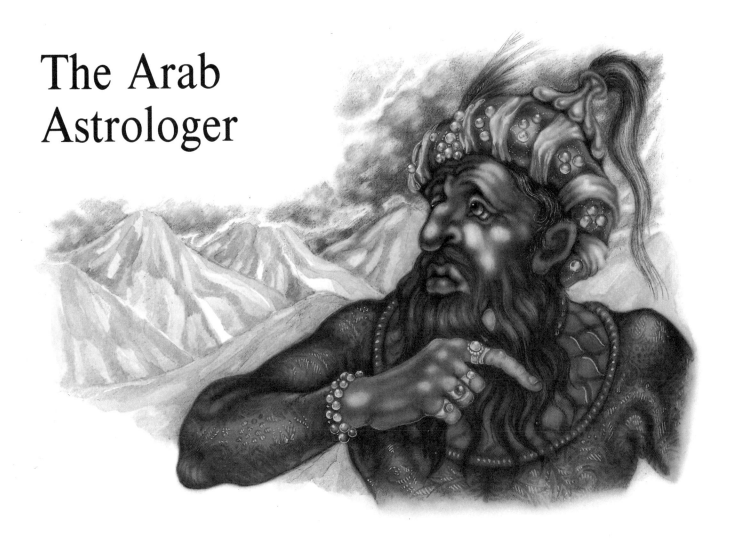

In the days when Southern Spain was still in the hands of African Moors, the city of Granada and its wide environs were ruled by Emir Aben Habuz. Old age was already assailing his head and cheeks with grey hair and whiskers, and all the ruler now wished for was to spend the autumn of his life in peace and quiet, and to enjoy its beauties.

However, in the north of his mountainous realm rebellion was brewing among the knights and princes whom he had once badly maltreated. They had not forgotten Habuz's cruelty or the fact that the land of Granada had once belonged to their grandfathers. They professed God the Father and Jesus his son, not Allah and Mohamed his Prophet as the noble Moor did. The Spaniards had white complexion, twisted moustaches, and a great desire to fight.

Hardly a day passed without their slipping by

some hidden mountain hollow or pass through the chain of Emir's guards. Then they sacked a rich manor, took prisoners, and, equally un-observed, returned with their booty to their strongholds on the other side of the mountains.

Their unrelenting attacks did not allow Emir Habuz a moment of peace. 'The city of Granada lies in the hollow under the mountains as though caught in a trap. What will happen should the Spaniards descend from their mountain precipices one day? Before Granada's garrison gets over the shock, they will have occupied the whole city including my palace. They will put me in prison, and will make themselves lords over the whole land of Granada.'

With such despair did the Emir muse, as he looked out towards the ragged mountain ridges with ever growing anxiety. They seemed to him to loom over the city as a threat; if only he could know at least half a day in advance should the enemy plan an assault from those parts!

In those days which were full of worry and sadness, a man with a white beard reaching down to his girdle appeared in the court. He declared himself to be a physician travelling from the distant land of Egypt. However, the long, richly ornamented staff which he wielded in his right hand suggested that he was initiated into astrology and the secret sciences. The staff was painted over with magic symbols from its twisted head to its metal tip. Even if he had not carried the magical staff, his piercing eyes bore testimony to his powers.

The learned Ibrahim, for that was the man's name, had the reputation of being able to make an elixir for eternal life and to read the stars. Of course, Emir Habuz did not hesitate to offer such a distinguished guest a whole suite of the most beautiful chambers in his palace. However, Ibrahim in all politeness declined the offer. He asked the Emir to allow him to settle down in a cave situated in the slope of a rise located very near the city. The Emir agreed. Thereupon Ibrahim had a roomy hall hewn out with a round opening in the ceiling for observing the stars. The most skilled artisans in the city supplied hitherto unseen instruments, alembics and flasks made of brass, copper, and glass.

The Emir was fond of visiting the cave and watched with curiosity how the work was going, even though he had very little understanding of what it was all about.

'You have had really wonderful things made,' he said to Ibrahim one day, with a deep sigh. 'Those that are directed towards the hole in the ceiling will allow you I presume to forecast the motions of the stars. I myself am not granted even the knowledge of what is happening in the mountains behind the city. I know neither the day nor the hour when the enemy may assault me from there.'

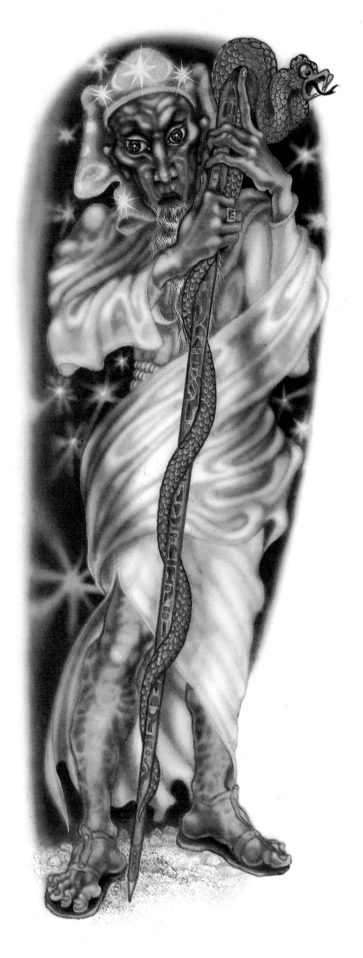

Ibrahim's eyes flashed as if he had been expecting this kind of speech for a long time. He opened an ebony casket which hung on the wall, and took out a thick roll of papyrus.

'This comes from an ancient Pharaoh's tomb,' he said. 'One day I rendered the King of Egypt a valuable service by my prophecy. In reward he allowed me to enter one of the pyramids and break the seal on the door of the death chamber where the mummy of an ancient pharaoh is laid to rest. From the treasures with which it is surrounded I was allowed to take as much as my servants could carry in their arms. However, I left my servants in the corridor and took nothing but this roll which was hidden in the darkest corner. I was not mistaken in my choice, for it contains drawings and instructions for making the most marvellous instruments. With the help of some of these I presume even your enemy can be rendered harmless.'

'If you manage that,' cried the Emir, 'I will fulfil even your boldest desire.'

The astrologer bowed as a sign of thanks, and set to work without delay. Before long there grew up under the hands of the ruler's masons a round tower made of stones which had been imported from Egypt.

Ibrahim placed on its top a brass statue of a rider with sword drawn. As long as peace prevailed in the mountains the rider's face remained turned towards the city. However, no sooner did the Spaniards appear anywhere, even in the most perfectly hidden hollow, the statue turned like a weathercock with its sword pointing to the exact spot. Thus the Emir of Granada no longer had need to fear of being caught unawares.

An even greater marvel was that he did not have to send a single soldier to fight the foe. Indeed, it was enough to enter the circular tower chamber whose windows looked out into all points of the globe. Under each of them a polished metal plate was fixed with an army of little ebony figures. Both infantry and horse, bowmen, lancers . . . even the standard-bearer and the drummer were to be found among them. In the middle of the chamber on a little table lay a wand written over with exotic characters.

'Take the wand in your fingers and be ready,' Ibrahim ordered the Emir when he had led him into the chamber for the first time. The bronze rider on the roof had just turned towards the

de Lope Pass and the wizard hurried to the window with a view in that direction.

'Look,' he said to the ruler and pointed to the figures on the plate underneath the window. The Emir stood dumbfounded: the figures had begun to move as though alive. Horses with riders were rearing up, soldiers were cleaning their weapons, and the air quivered with a faint buzzing which recalled the rolling of war drums.

'It looks as if your enemies were preparing for a big attack,' said the astrologer. 'If you are unwilling to shed blood in a battle, you can put them to flight from this very chamber,' he said, and he asked the ruler to use the wand to disperse and tumble the figures.

'Now, send out patrols on the fastest horses to travel to the de Lope Pass. Let them report back as soon as possible as to what they have seen with their own eyes,' he said with a smile. 'They can leave their weapons behind, for they shall not need them.'

When the patrols returned from the mountains they reported how an incomprehensible confusion had arisen in the enemy camp, and how one side started skirmishes against the other until at last they ran helter skelter back from where they had come. The Emir recalled the tiny toppled figures in the tower.

'Ibrahim is not only a wizard, he is a magician of magicians and a magus of magi,' he said to himself, his soul flooding with awesome fear mingled with joy.

Before long Ibrahim asked whether he might extend his cave residence by further chambers.

'Allah be thanked that the astrologer has taken a fancy to my court,' the ruler bowed to the ground in spirit and he did not spare money to ensure that the wizard's rock residence should be equipped with the greatest magnificence possible.

Thanks to the bronze rider and the magic tower chamber he had no further need to worry about the rebellious Spaniards. All he had to do to rout the enemy was to use the wand and topple the ebony figures. At last the time came when he was able to enjoy comfort and beauties of the world in quiet and peace. Leaning against soft pillows he now took delight in listening to the playing of the lute in which a Christian princess whom soldiers had brought to his court as a prisoner excelled. The Emir listened with ever growing dedication not only to her instrument, but even to her proud counsels and wishes.

'The princess is complaining that the walls and vaults of my palace are frustrating her play with its echoes,' he said to Ibrahim one day. 'I know that you can do the incredible. Build a seat for her and myself which will exceed in beauty all Moorish castles and palaces.'

'Woe betide the ruler who succumbs to the whims of a youthful maiden,' pronounced the wizard sternly. 'You are not so old yet, Emir Habuz, that you may afford to put aside your ruler's duties in favour of idle pleasures.'

'Build me a palace according to my wishes,

and if you desire half of my realm in return you shall have it,' said the Emir, and his eyes flashed with single-minded lust.

For a while the astrologer kept silent, and then he shrugged his shoulders:

'All right, you shall have that, but instead of a half of your realm I ask for something else. Promise me that I shall have the first horse that passes through the main gate of your courtyard. The first horse including the load.'

'You shall have it,' cried the Emir pleasantly surprised by his modesty, 'and now down to work for I am burning with impatience.'

The site Ibrahim chose for the castle was the hilltop where he had his own cave. Before long, under his guidance the walls began to rise, and behind them the roofs of the palace resplendent with gold. An impressive gate guarded the entrance, and above it the astrologer engraved a giant key with a giant hand. Thereupon he delivered an incantation in an unknown tongue, and descending into his rocky chambers shut himself off from the world.

Some days later, the ruler received an invitation to inspect the construction. The very next morning he came riding there accompanied by the Princess on a magnificently bedecked white horse, a silver lute hanging on her young white neck. The astrologer, leaning on his staff, was already waiting before the gate.

'The key and the hand,' said Ibrahim, pointing to the engraved symbols, 'protect the access to the castle. Until the hand seizes the key, nothing untoward can befall anyone living upon this hill.'

Then something quite unexpected happened. While the Emir, in his curiosity, was examining the stone talismans, the Princess's white horse reared up, and before the others knew what had happened it ran inside through the gate.

'Look, Emir, there is the reward you have promised me,' cried the astrologer. 'The white horse with a harness set with precious stones, and the load it bears in the saddle: the maiden with the silver lute!'

In vain did the ruler promise, in exchange for the Princess, as much gold and jewellery from his treasures as the strongest mule could carry for Ibrahim would not back down, and when at last he reminded the Moorish ruler that it would be an outrage for him not to keep his word, Emir Habuz flew into a rage and showered the wizard with a hail of insults.

'So rule your unfortunate realm by yourself. I will just laugh at you from my underground residence,' answered Ibrahim and snapped his fingers. At that moment the white steed with the Princess came running like an obedient little dog. The astrologer seized him by the rein, struck the earth with his staff and the earth opened wide, all the three vanishing into its depths.

The enraged Emir rushed to the cave entrance at the head of his men-at-arms, but there was nothing left of the opening. All that faced the pursuers was a solid wall of rock.

When the ruler returned to his old palace, he saw the bronze rider just turning in the direction of the astrologer's hill. He gazed in that direction, and for a moment he stood transfixed: the whole structure which Ibrahim had created vanished as though it had been a vision!

That day was the beginning of bad times for Habuz's realm. The rider on the tower never moved an inch again. Never again did it turn to point with his sword towards the attacker, and so the Spaniards were able to pester the land with unexpected raids. In the end Emir Habuz, beset with worries about his throne, died.

All that was left of the astrologer's magic castle was the gate with the key and the hand and the castle ramparts. People began to call it 'the King's folly', and that appellation was the only reminder of the foolish Emir to remain in their memory.

However, years after in that very spot, on the As-Sabika hilltop near Granada, one of the loveliest buildings of ancient Spain came to be built: the palace and fortress of Alhambra. The stone hand and the key adorning the main entrance can be seen there even today.

To this day people say that on warm summer nights if one stands by that gate the sound of a lute and a maiden's soft singing can be heard from somewhere under the earth. It is the captive Princess who still lulls to sleep the Arab astrologer with music and song, and whom the great magus still holds in his power in the magnificent chambers inside the rock which forms the base of Alhambra. For no one can resist the sound enough not to let himself be lulled into sweet dreams.

How Falkenstein Castle Got Its Name

To this day the countryside near the upper reaches of the Dreisam River is one of the finest nooks of the Black Forest. In the places where the river pass drops down into a gorge of such a depth that it has earned the name of the 'Hell Gorge', it is rather a rugged beauty.

In the days of the iron knights of the Crusades the gorge was guarded by a castle of which nothing but a ragged ruin has remained. At the time when it was the seat of Knight Kuno and his wife Ida, however, its tower and the palace shone white in the sea of the neighbouring woods, and was so new that it did not even have a name.

'These woods around us are like green walls,' Kuno said to his spouse one day, sighing. 'I feel more like a prisoner than a ruler. My desire is to see lands which are the hunting grounds of long-maned lions, like our neighbour, Knight Engelbert who has just returned from a Crusade.'

'Don't leave me, my dear Kuno,' sobbed Ida.

'A true knight should perform a great deed for the mistress of his heart. I have heard that a monk reached the spot where the world has its end, where the sky touches the earth. When he put his head through a crack of which there are plenty in the canopy of heaven, he beheld truly incredible sights: eternally flaming fires, the leather bellows from which the winds blow, and even the giant wheels that make the Sun, the Moon and the stars go round. I do not wish just to wander about like the monk, but to pluck you a star for your tiara, Ida!'

'Once again I beseech you, do not leave me,' sobbed the lady, tears filling her eyes.

The knight was greatly moved by such a show of devotion, and broke his wedding ring into two halves, giving one half to Ida.

'My dear wife, the journey to the end of the world and back to you is sure to be a long one. Before we rejoin the two halves of the ring, as many as seven years may pass. If by that time I do not return it will mean that I have been made captive by heathens, or that I am dead. If a worthy man asks for your hand, do not hesitate to marry him. Do not stay here alone, with no-one to love you or care for you.'

'Please, do not talk like that, Kuno, you only make my sorrow harder to bear,' answered Ida. She had come to realize that not even tears would move a knight who had resolved to do a great deed.

The next day Kuno, together with three of his retainers rode out of the castle gate clad in only light armour, wearing no helmet or sword, and with only a dagger in his belt.

'We are not going to war, but on a search for knowledge,' he told his men-at-arms, pointing to the sun which had just risen above the hill-tops. 'Over there is the Orient! They say that the World's End which lies behind it borders on Paradise itself!'

After a long journey the four riders finally arrived at the port of Taranto on the Ionian Sea. At that time there was only one ship bound for the Syrian city of Antioch, Kuno's destination. The moment they approached it the horses began to rear up wildly, and Kuno's men saw this as an ill omen; but Kuno boarded the ship with a firm stride, and so his retainers were bound to follow.

It was not without reason that the horses took fright in Taranto. As they were nearing the end of the voyage, a terrible gale arose on the sea. It drove the ship farther and farther off its course until it was cast up on the rocks of an unknown and deserted shore. A giant wave tossed the knight out upon the beach like a mussel shell.

After a while, when he had recovered from the shock, he began to look around for the ship and his retainers but all in vain. So he sat down among the pebbles, head in hands. As he mused over his misfortune, the storm slowly subsided and in the stillness he heard no other sound but a strange whisper, 'Rise and journey on. Are you not eager to reach the World's End? It lies ahead of you, so hurry up, my dear!'

Kuno looked round in despair, but all he could see was the ocean and some rocks. At that moment he seemed more like a frightened tramp than a brave knight, nevertheless he roused himself and stepped out to explore the unknown land.

After some time he found himself in a country full of gorges, and overgrown with thorny bushes. He sat down on a boulder filled with despair just as before on the seashore. Suddenly, he sprang to his feet to the touch of a hand

on his shoulders. For a moment he thought he was dreaming, for there before him stood his three retainers, safe and sound!

'This is wonderful; now our expedition is sure to be a success,' said the delighted Kuno. 'We shall set out with a renewed will, even though from now on we have only our own legs to rely on. We are standing on the soil of the Orient, and our destination is not far.'

So they set out marching. The countryside turned into a wilderness which was becoming increasingly arid, and the animals which they had been hunting for food as they went were getting scarcer and scarcer. None of the travellers was able to tell how long they had been trudging through these unknown lands. Was it months or perhaps years that passed? There was no choice but to go on until exhausted, they collapsed from hunger and thirst.

Suddenly, they heard an animal howling in the distance. Was it a steppe wolf or a jackal? 'Even if it is the king of the wild beasts, he cannot live here without water,' mused Kuno, and he raised himself on his elbows with a new hope stirring in his heart. The next moment he was rubbing his eyes with wonder to chase away the vision that had appeared before him. However, the hallucination would not go. Instead of rocks and hills there was a desert of sands smoother than a lake with no wind rippling its surface, and in the desert, stretching from one end of the horizon to the other, there was a white wall as high as the ramparts of a fortress.

'This is where our journey ends,' the armed men exclaimed. 'That wall is indeed the end of the world, your Grace!'

Thus Kuno persuaded himself that what he saw was no illusion, and his eyes shone eagerly.

'Climb up,' he told Walter, who was the nimblest of them, 'and report everything you see behind the wall.'

Walter the retainer, using the chinks between the stones easily climbed up to the very top, but instead of turning back to his companions and

telling them what he saw, he burst into a devilish laughter. All that those on the ground saw was how he stretched his arms and jumped over to the other side.

So Kuno sent up Udo, the second of his retainers, to find out what had happened to Walter. Once up there however, Udo did just the same as Walter had done before him, and with a devilish laugh disappeared behind the wall as though down a trapdoor.

It was with a heavy heart that Kuno sent up the last, the oldest retainer called Helg. In spite of his age Helg climbed up nimbly, but even he, the truest of the true, once at the top behaved just the same as the two men before him.

'It is my turn now,' whispered the knight gaining a hold with his fingertips in the first crack between the stones, but fell back down to the ground nearly breaking his neck. The wall burned like a devil's furnace. So that was the reason why it shone with such whiteness, the stones were burning with a white heat.

Before he could recover his senses, a black and red hairy head appeared above the wall. Who else could it have belonged to but to the devil himself?

'You are about to look at the end of the world, and while doing so you have forgotten all about your Ida!' laughed the devil (for that is who it was), in the same way as the armed men had done just before they disappeared behind the wall. 'Do you not remember that tomorrow it'll be seven years since you said goodbye to her at the castle gate? Your gentle spouse will celebrate her wedding with another man, she is just fulfilling your wish, Sir knight! She takes you for a dead man, and has already had candles lit for the office of the dead.'

Kuno was dumbstruck. So it was seven whole years since he had first set out on his journey.

'For heaven's sake, get me back to my castle before the wedding takes place!' he shouted at the devil. 'Rich shall be my reward, I will not stint.'

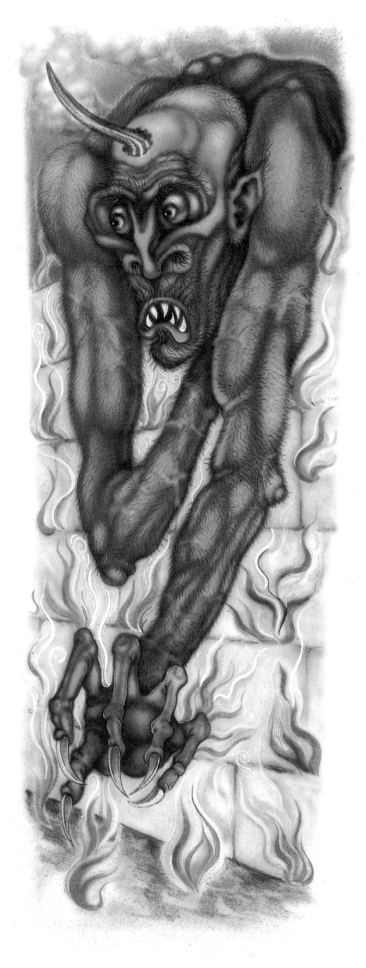

'You shall reward me with your soul then,' answered the voice behind the wall.

The knight's eyes were downcast.

'It is no small thing you are asking,' he said after a while, 'but let it be so. I would rather lose my soul than my dearly beloved Ida. I have but one wish and it is that you take my soul when I fall asleep during the journey. I do not wish to be conscious at such a terrible moment.'

'All right,' said the devil. For he saw how that human worm down there at the foot of the wall could hardly stand on his legs; he would fall asleep even before they reached the sea in flight. So the devil carved everything they had agreed on into a stone tablet and dropped it at Kuno's feet. Then he ordered him, 'Cut your little finger and sign the covenant with your blood!'

The moment Kuno had done this the ground parted and from the chasm burst a green flame which smelled of sulphur and threw out, just in front of the knight, a giant lion with the wings of a bat. 'Get on my back, there is no time to lose!' cried the lion. The knight mounted the lion as though it were a horse and the animal swung his tail, waved his wings, and rose into the air taking Kuno high into the sky.

How slow the flight seemed across the monotonous expanse of the sea! Later on when they flew into a cloud which enveloped them with grey semi-darkness, Kuno could no longer keep awake. His head sank in drowsiness as the

devil's howling laughter echoed in the distance. However, the devil's delight at the thought that Kuno was asleep proved premature. The devil, who could see even a little mouse beyond the seven seas, could not fail to notice the wings of a great falcon which emerged from the clouds and now circled round Kuno's head. The bird circled again, even nearer, so near that his wings slapped the knight's forehead, nose and temples. Kuno came to at once, and was hard put to it to defend himself against the falcon's attacks.

From the distance where only a moment before the triumphant laughter had resounded now came a raging howl. The devil was infuriated by his defeat and he realized that the falcon would not let Kuno fall asleep until the flight was over.

Before long the bird of prey vanished into the blue sky and the knight breathed a sigh of relief and joy. Down below him the sea had changed colour. It was now the emerald green of the Black Forest woods that he knew so well. There, across the silver river he noticed the tower of his own castle! In flight as silent as a bat, the lion lighted near the rear tower wall, where he threw Kuno off his back and was then swallowed up by the earth.

Meanwhile, the people in the castle were busy with happy tasks, for before noon that very day the noble lady was to celebrate her wedding as she had been advised by her husband who had failed to return.

On a wedding day every person that passes through the castle gate is a welcome guest. Doubly welcome was the pilgrim who said he had come all the way from the Holy Sepulchre in the Holy Land. In places where his face was not overgrown with a beard it had the colour of bronze, so dark had it become from the burning sun in foreign lands. Kuno was conducted to the banqueting hall and the deathly pale bride, honouring an old custom, handed him a cup of white wine.

The unknown guest lifted the cup to his lips, drank his hostess's health and happiness, and then he put his own half of the wedding ring into the empty cup saying: 'My lady, please accept a small present in return for your kind hospitality.'

Ida glanced into the cup and then she looked into the guest's eyes. At that moment her head began to swim, and with tears and happy smiles she sank into her husband's arms. 'Kuno, my darling, you have come back just in time!'

As though summoned by her cry the sturdy falcon once again flew down from the sky and circled above the heads of the husband and wife who were reunited after suffering so many hardships. Of all the adventures he had experienced the first that Kuno recounted to Ida was how up in the clouds the falcon did not let him fall asleep and so saved his soul from hell.

Thereupon after his happy return Kuno and his beloved Ida lived on for many long years, and out of gratitude to the falcon, his saviour, he had the falcon's likeness depicted in his coat of arms and called his seat Falkenstein — the Falcon Castle.

Wild Jane

On the northern edge of the plain around the Bulgarian towns of Pazardzik and Plovdiv, in places where the Sredna Gora mountain range towers to gigantic heights, icy waters roll along the boulder-filled bed in a river which bears a girl's name. An old legend tells us how it came to be so.

When the Turks invaded the Bulgarian land bent on subjugating its people, their mounted hosts who came in far superior numbers flooded only the plains extending around the big rivers. As for the mountains, they did not dare to enter them. The mountain tops as well as the hillsides bristled with towers and dented battlements of strongly fortified guard-castles.

The Turks were averse to dismounting from their fast horses and climbing up the break-neck paths under the walls of fortresses in an effort to capture them.

Thus it happened that even Dushkovchenin and Krasen, the mightiest of the chain of castles along the wildly running river, were spared. Dushkovchenin guarded a pass beyond which the river left the mountains, and it was indeed

hard to tell which of the keeps and walls was part of the rocks and which of them had been constructed by human hand. Krasen Castle towered above the pointed top of a steep mountain farther on, in the direction of the valley, and was no less impregnable than Dushkovchenin Castle.

Their owners were just as powerful as the castles themselves. Wide pasture-lands full of cattle and forests teeming with deer were part of both estates, and so the lords of the castles had no reason to envy each other. They even had luck with their children: the merry, indomitable Jane, daughter of the Krasen noble, had grown into the most beautiful maiden in the land, and Boris, the young master of Dushkovchenin, matured into a noble-minded gentleman.

In spite of all this good fortune, as though through the working of the devil himself, both fathers bore each other a spiteful grudge. Now that the Turks were penetrating ever farther into the land, all and sundry at the neighbouring castles were hoping that the two would finally give up their unnecessary disputes and hold out

their hands in an offer of peace. For indeed, there was no time to lose in making preparations to defend their castles against their common enemy.

This did not happen, however. The lord of Krasen Castle did not cease looking up to the rich Greek merchants who had settled in the venerable city of Plovdiv. He kept visiting them even though the city had been occupied by the Turks — either to borrow gold coins to buy a new horse, or else to play dice for high stakes.

On the other hand, the noble of Dushkovchenin counted the Greeks among his mortal enemies, and it was this very fact that remained the bitterest apple of discord between them.

'Foreigners are bringing our land to ruin, and it is indeed immaterial whether it is caused by the Turks and their sabres and the hoofs of their cavalry, or by the Greeks and their bloodsucking business deals. That traitor of Krasen Castle has forgotten he is a Bulgarian, and is making friends with them!' complained the lord of Dushkovchenin Castle to the heavens and to his neighbours' ears.

Thus there was no love lost between their fathers, but not so between their children. Boris and Jane had loved each other since they were little children and now, as they grew up, they fell in love. They met but rarely and then it was in secret so that their fathers should not find out. Despite all this they cherished a hope that they would celebrate their wedding one day when the two families were reconciled.

So time passed. One day the lord of Krasen returned from Plovdiv in such an excellent mood that even the guard at the gate wondered at it.

'You must have had a great success in your dice,' observed Jane when they met at the dinner table. She genuinely thought that her father had had a stroke of luck and was pleased with an unexpected sum of money.

'A great success? Yes, indeed, a great success for both you and me; you might call it that!'

said the lord of Krasen Castle laughing till the belt on his girdle bobbed up and down. 'The richest Greek in Plovdiv has asked for your hand, go and prepare your trousseau.'

Should a stone ball from a Turkish catapult have flown through the window straight on to the dinner table at that exact moment, Jane could not have been more astounded. However, since she excelled in resolve as much as in grace, she had an answer ready, 'I am not going to marry a town merchant, father, even if he should sit on all the treasures of the world. Send him word he should not waste his time with the wooing.'

'Since when is it a habit at Krasen to oppose the will of its master?' rejoined the nobleman turning red in the face with rage. 'Yesterday I gave my word, tomorrow his matchmakers are coming to the castle!'

Jane did not say another word. However, that very night she tied her things into a bundle, slipped through a secret gate out of Krasen, and

fled along the mountain paths to Dushkovchenin Castle. Its master received her like his own daughter, and Boris as his own beloved bride.

However, the lord of Krasen Castle had enough anger upon which to feed seven Hells when he learnt of her flight. The walls of the pass echoed his curses on his daughter and the whole of Dushkovchenin Castle. Now he hated his neighbour like poison, and the furious rage had clouded his senses. As though he had forgotten all the evil which the Turks had brought upon his land, he set off for the town of Pazardzik to see the Turkish governor.

Nor did he beg, he a Bulgarian nobleman, anything of less weight than that the Turks help in capturing and routing the Dushkovchenin! The Bey of Pazardzik could hardly contain himself from whooping aloud for it was just what he had expected! He had long been preparing to assault Dushkovchenin, for this castle was the greatest obstacle to the Turks' entry into the mountains. It was through the mountains that

the Turks had to pass if they wanted to reach the fertile plains to the north of the Danube.

Until then no one had even thought of conquering such a mighty castle — all the more so since the equally strongly fortified castle of Krasen stood nearby. Indeed, Krasen's garrison could have so easily come at the attackers of Dushkovchenin from the rear. Now its lord and commander sought Turkish help against Dushkovchenin and the Turkish governor could scarcely believe his good fortune.

The third day, as agreed, the Turks together with the garrison of Krasen marched out against Dushkovchenin from both sides at the same time. Before the defenders of the castle recovered from the shock the attackers stood underneath the walls. The lord of Krasen knew the weak points of the castle very well, having been a frequent guest there before the two noblemen fell foul of each other, so it was not long before the Turks' battering rams pierced the walls and the enemy rushed inside.

The defenders fought like lions even though they knew at the outset that the battle was lost.

Jane never left the side of her Boris, and conducted herself in the thick of battle just like the others. The fighting did not cease even after the lord of the castle had fallen dead to the ground for Boris took over the command. It was only after he had been badly injured and all that was left of the Dushkovchenin garrison were but a faithful few who were sure to find nothing but death in further fighting that Jane persuaded them to retreat. With Boris, whom two of the strongest men carried on their shoulders the defenders succeeded in escaping through a secret postern. Beyond it lay dense forest. The fugitives silently vanished into its hidden depths like a procession of wood spirits.

The lord of Krasen searched every corner of the conquered Dushkovchenin for his daughter, but in vain. It was as though she had vanished into thin air.

'What was my revenge worth?' he whispered over the body of the lord of Dushkovchenin who had once been his friend. As he looked about the smoking ruins which had yesterday been a proud Bulgarian castle, the lord of Krasen sobbed bitterly.

However, he was destined to learn to his dismay who was to benefit from the revenge: the Bey of Pazardzik struck while the iron was hot.

'The castle is uprooted as you had wished,' he said to his ally the moment the work of ruin had been accomplished. 'And your worthy neighbour has turned up his toes. Don't you think it is time for you to show your gratitude for my help? The soldiers are tired, the wounded need their wounds dressed. Don't they deserve a bit of rest at your castle?'

The Bulgarian nobleman had no choice but to agree, and so the Turks entered the gates of Krasen unopposed. At once they made them-

selves at home in the castle, and did not show any readiness to leave even a week later. They feasted merrily on the castle's provisions, and it was only after not a crumb was left in the larders that the bey informed his host that he was going back to Pazardzik. 'You had better come along yourself,' he told the lord of the castle as he sat on his horse, about to leave.

'Why should I leave my home?' asked the astonished nobleman. 'My daughter Jane, my only comfort in these times, is sure to come back under her native roof.'

'Just turn round and look up at your native roofs!' cried the bey with a grin, and he set spurs to his horse and was gone.

The earth trembled beneath the nobleman's feet: smoke was pouring from the roofs of Krasen, flames were already blazing through the tiles, and the spire of the main tower was aflame like an enormous torch. The Turks had set fire to his castle!

Thus the treason and revenge he had carried out against his neighbour turned back on the one who had committed them. Like a madman the lord of Krasen rushed into the wrecked gate of the palace behind which a fiery furnace was roaring. He was never seen again.

Meanwhile, in the best of spirits the Turkish governor led his cavalry back to Pazardzik. It was no wonder he was so happy, for he had managed to kill two birds with one stone: two of the most powerful castles in the foothills lay in ruins, the road to the north was open at last! He had a good reason to rejoice, and yet his joy was to be shortlived!

In a mountain chalet high above the river Jane was nursing her dear Boris for the wounds he had suffered in the battle for Duchkovchen-

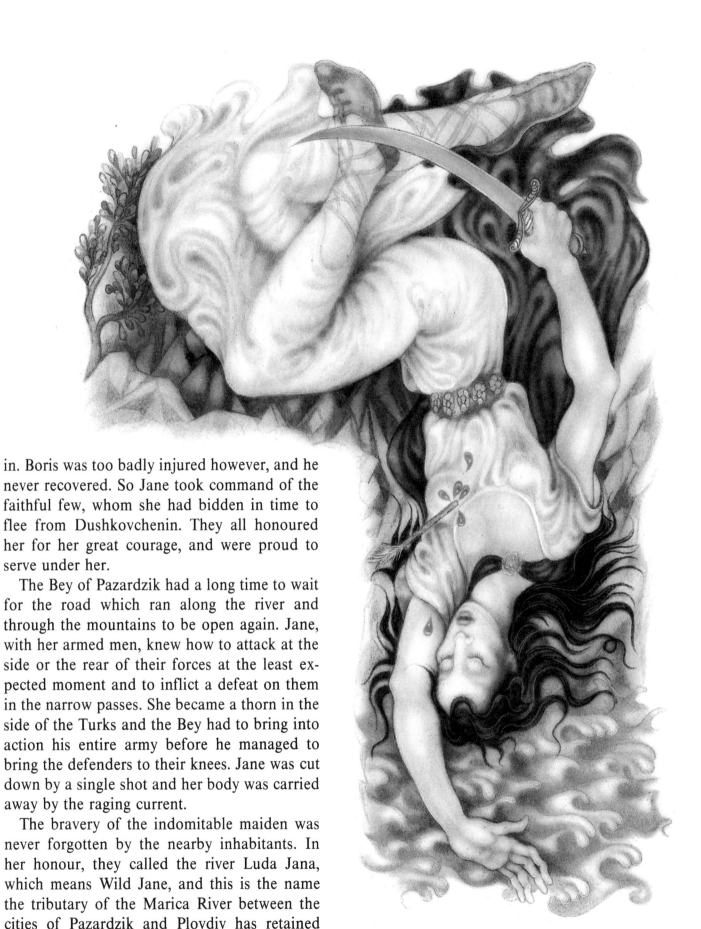

in. Boris was too badly injured however, and he never recovered. So Jane took command of the faithful few, whom she had bidden in time to flee from Dushkovchenin. They all honoured her for her great courage, and were proud to serve under her.

The Bey of Pazardzik had a long time to wait for the road which ran along the river and through the mountains to be open again. Jane, with her armed men, knew how to attack at the side or the rear of their forces at the least expected moment and to inflict a defeat on them in the narrow passes. She became a thorn in the side of the Turks and the Bey had to bring into action his entire army before he managed to bring the defenders to their knees. Jane was cut down by a single shot and her body was carried away by the raging current.

The bravery of the indomitable maiden was never forgotten by the nearby inhabitants. In her honour, they called the river Luda Jana, which means Wild Jane, and this is the name the tributary of the Marica River between the cities of Pazardzik and Plovdiv has retained to this day.

The Well at Mukachevo Castle

The ancient Castle of Mukachevo stands on a peculiar site: it rises on the hill of Lovalec from a plain as flat as a table top. It lies south of the river Latorica, half an hour's walk from the town of Mukachevo. The hill stands quite alone on the plain so all who see it immediately wonder how it came to be there.

'Who knows, it might even have been carried across from the opposite bank along with the castle by a pack of devils of the Latorica,' local people would say. 'Just look how many hills and mountains rise on the northern side of the river, even as far as the ridges of the Carpathians. The devil spoils all he can. Why should he not spoil a lovely lowland when he had so many hills at hand on the other side of the river?'

In this way Mukachevo Castle had, from its very foundation, been associated with foul intrigues and spiteful acts of the devil.

Centuries passed until one summer the castle became the seat of Prince Fyodor Koryatovich. The nobleman was very fond of hearing people say of him that he was a man of gentle disposition but one of resolution, and so the castle was in for busy times. The first thing the Prince did was to have new stone walls built.

He contemplated them with satisfaction, until he looked at the road rising towards the castle, and knit his brows with indignation. There was a carriage carrying a big barrel jerking along the road, drawn by a team of oxen. It was but one of the many barrels that had to be brought up to the castle day by day. All it contained was water from the village down in the fields. Mukachevo Castle, which looked so impregnable, had no well of its own.

What did it matter how high the walls were? If the castle were under siege, not even a fox let alone a water waggon would be able to slip through the enemy lines. Everybody in the castle would die of thirst!

As the Prince was not fond of delays he immediately bade his burgrave appear before him and ordered a well to be sunk in the courtyard.

From that day on all the men who had been building the walls and moat began to sink a shaft into the rock.

It was slow work. The rock offered great resistance, and chisels and cutters shattered frequently. The depth of the well increased only inch by inch, and still no water appeared. The only thing to moisten the walls of the shaft were the trickles of sweat shed by the men at their unrelenting toil.

In vain did the Prince call upon new strong men from far and wide to help them; they had tunnelled the whole hill from top to bottom, but of water there was no trace. So the noble Koryatovich ordered men to hew down to the very base of the rock, and every day when the sun stood at its highest in the sky he would come to the shaft and search its depths with his eyes. Every time it looked just the same as it had the day before: nothing but sheer black darkness in which not a single drop glittered.

'This is certainly the work of the very devil!' he exclaimed in the end, beside himself with anger and rage. 'Enough of vain toil!', and he ordered his herald to make a proclamation all over the land: 'Whoever makes water appear in the Mukachevo Castle well shall be rewarded by Prince Fyodor Koryatovich with a sack of ducats!'

He did not have to wait long. The very next day there appeared in the castle a gnome with a nose so long and bent that it nearly dug a furrow in the earth, and with a face as dirty as though he had just left a charcoal pile. His coat and trousers had a gentlemanly cut though, and there was a falcon's feather stuck in his fur-trimmed cap, even longer than the mannikin himself.

'Humble servant of Your Royal Grace,' he said swinging his cap around in greeting in a way not to be outdone by the court barber-surgeon himself. 'It has come to my ears that you have promised a sack of gold to anyone able to fill your castle well with water. Is it true?'

'Do you think I am a liar?' frowned the Prince.

'Nowadays you cannot believe even a dead man that he has died,' croaked the mannikin. 'Never mind though. Where is that well of yours without any water in it?' The moment they led the goblin to the shaft he lifted the tails of his coat, and without ceremony jumped inside. Immediately afterwards one could hear bubbling and seething in the depth, then a hissing sound was heard, followed by dark rumbling, and the smell of sulphur rose from the shaft. A moment later, the gnome's head appeared over the edge of the well.

'It's done!' he cried when he had climbed out and shaken drops of water out of his coat-tails.

The Prince was dumbfounded and so were all those who peered down the shaft: there was indeed water in the hole.

'Get the gold ready, Fyodor Koryatovich! In three days and three nights I will come and fetch it!' croaked the big-nose instead of saying goodbye.

So the castle now had water, but still somehow its inhabitants were not satisfied. Rumours passed from ear to ear about the goblin's black magic, but the water for the castle was there, and so everyone heaved a sigh of relief in the end. Only Prince Koryatovich looked as though he had drunk a proper draught of vinegar. With his hands behind his back he passed through

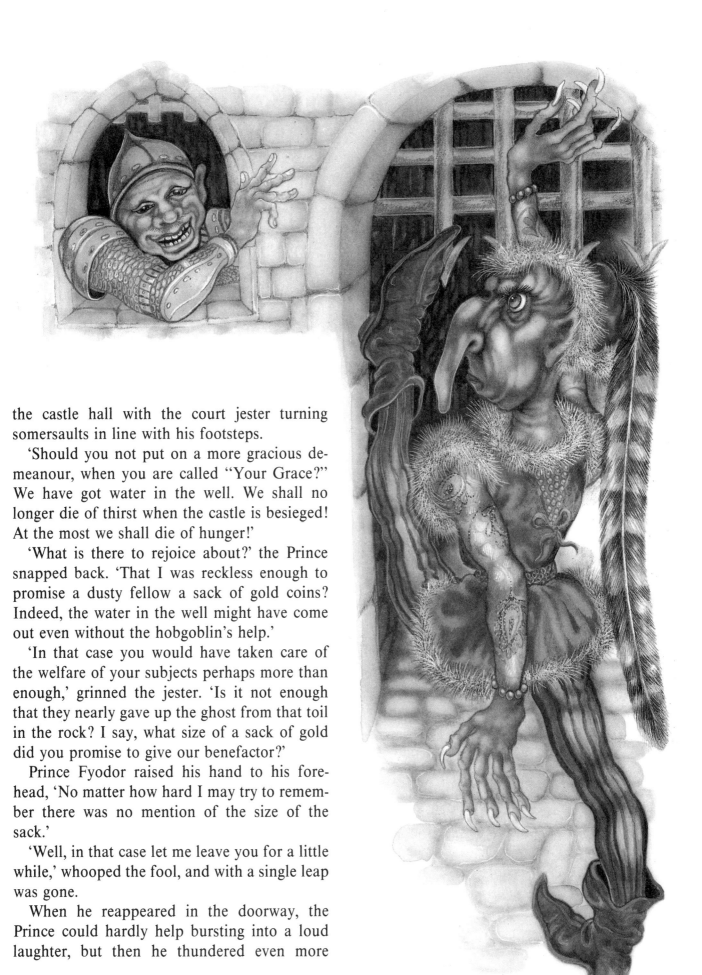

the castle hall with the court jester turning somersaults in line with his footsteps.

'Should you not put on a more gracious demeanour, when you are called "Your Grace?" We have got water in the well. We shall no longer die of thirst when the castle is besieged! At the most we shall die of hunger!'

'What is there to rejoice about?' the Prince snapped back. 'That I was reckless enough to promise a dusty fellow a sack of gold coins? Indeed, the water in the well might have come out even without the hobgoblin's help.'

'In that case you would have taken care of the welfare of your subjects perhaps more than enough,' grinned the jester. 'Is it not enough that they nearly gave up the ghost from that toil in the rock? I say, what size of a sack of gold did you promise to give our benefactor?'

Prince Fyodor raised his hand to his forehead, 'No matter how hard I may try to remember there was no mention of the size of the sack.'

'Well, in that case let me leave you for a little while,' whooped the fool, and with a single leap was gone.

When he reappeared in the doorway, the Prince could hardly help bursting into a loud laughter, but then he thundered even more

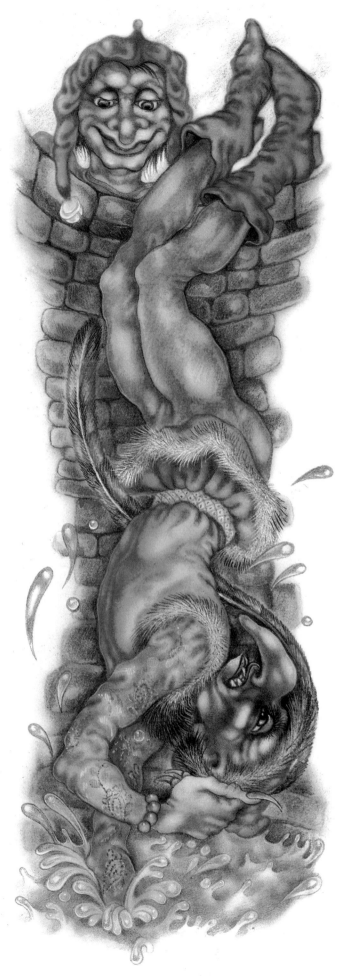

loudly, 'Believe me, I am in no mood at present to watch your tomfoolery in what looks like an old woman's rags!'

They were no old woman's rags the jester was wearing, however; he was in fact wrapped round with empty sacks.

'I picked them up in the castle larder and in many other places besides — there are all kinds of sacks about, judge for yourself.'

Then, as though in a market place the fool started unfolding before the Prince bags so big that they could almost be used instead of sails to drive ships, sacks rather smaller from which clouds of flour were still floating, little sacks for lentil and peas, and finally tiny pouches of soft linen for spices. It was one of these tiny bags that the fool pointed at, 'This also belongs to the great family of sacks and pouches, and would probably not even hold ten gold coins. A tiny pouch of gold for a tiny goblin — indeed, the size was not mentioned at all.'

'Stop that. I am a nobleman, not a cheat,' said the Prince waving his hand angrily.

The Prince was unable to rest peacefully however, and the morning before the dwarf was due to return, a whisper ran amongst the servants that the master had been pacing up and down in his bedroom all night.

Was there any wonder? On the one hand, Prince Koryatovich was imagining the gold coins that he might save by cheating the gnome, and on the other hand, there was his nobleman's honour to uphold.

The next morning the gnome appeared in the castle hall as though he had flown right down the chimney. Prince Fyodor however, was ready to face him. Without a word he dropped a small linen pouch into the dwarf's palm, within which a few meagre coins tinkled.

'What is this supposed to mean?' said the mannikin all dumbfounded. 'We agreed on a sack of gold, do you not remember?'

'Well, this is it. There was no mention of the size of the sack,' replied the Prince.

'Oh, by the throne of Lucifer! Oh, by all the gates of Hell! Just look at our noble prince who is so fond of hearing it said that he is a charitable lord!'

By then the mannikin was jumping up to the ceiling like an enormous flea; and then with curses most horrible to witness he ran out to the well, and jumped straight in.

When he dropped onto the surface, there was a rumbling sound like a thump on a big drum. All this was nothing compared with the loud cursing and terrible swearing by which the gnome continued to vent his rage down below in the well.

People say that even to this day, from time to time, a strange muttering and babbling noise can be heard from the Mukachevo Castle well. Some say that is the sound of waters running deep beneath the ground. Others claim that the gnome is still unable to forget how he once swallowed Prince Fyodor's bait. He is wary of climbing back into the world of men, and prefers to give vent to his fury by remaining underground and cursing loudly.

The Stone Knight

To this day the Swiss castle of Waldenburg proudly looks down upon the little town below it as well as upon the valley stretching farther into the distance. At one time it had a master who was also proud: Knight John thought of nothing but riotous parties and revels. However, a merry mind in his subjects was not to his liking. His greatest joy was to see them shake with fear before him.

John of Waldenburg often found himself in a rather downcast mood however. Loneliness was what scared him in his huge, empty castle, and so he would often invite all the nobles from near and far to visit him. The tables in the banqueting hall groaned with the weight of choice dainties, and the wine flowed like a river, while in the cottages below the castle there was not so much as a crust of dry bread to be found. When John rode out to hunt, the woods would resound with boisterous fanfares and tally-hos, but in the fields labourers pined under the scourges of the knight's bailiffs.

On the very edge of the township at that time, there was a poor serf living in a miserable hovel with his wife and a fine flock of children. There were indeed many hungry mouths around the table; but how were the parents to feed them all when the cottier was forced to toil on the manorial fields in order to fill the rich knight's granaries?

No sooner had the winter snow vanished from the fields than he would plough, harrow, manure, sow and harvest alongside his fellow serfs from dawn to dusk. Only at night was he able to till his only little field. Month after month passed until it was nearly autumn. Hunger knocked at the door of the hovel, while the corn in the master's field grew overripe and began to shed grain. It was high time to reap it.

The knight had his field harvested to the very last ear, and so the cottier hoped that now at least a few days would certainly be left for him to tend the crops in his own little field. However, early in the morning, hardly had he honed his scythe than there was the bailiff banging at the door and shouting the lord's order for him to present himself at the castle without delay so as to carry stones for the new wing.

At that very moment the youngest child cried out with hunger and the cottier's eyes darkened with anger and rage. He seized an empty bowl from the shelf, pushed it into the bailiff's hand and cried, 'Go and tell the honourable knight to have this bowl filled at least once a day in his castle kitchen so that my family should not starve. Then I will come up to the castle as he demands. Otherwise he shall never see me there!'

The bailiff turned around and went, but some moments later he was back with two deputies. In vain did the wife beg, in vain did the children cry. The men-at-arms dragged the cottier off to the castle to face Knight John, who was beside himself with rage.

'To the dungeon with him, to the deepest cell in the tower! Let him talk about poverty with the toads,' Knight John commanded.

The cottier's wife and children waited in vain for their father to return home that day. Neither did he come the day after, nor in a week, nor for the whole of autumn either. Already the winter had been heralded in by the first snow. When they had eaten the last little loaf baked from the flour they had borrowed from neighbours, the cottier's wife sat down at the empty table, and tears came to her eyes.

'Don't cry, mother,' said the eldest son. 'We will go to the castle and beg our noble master to

let our father come home, and at once things will be better again.'

'Perhaps he will really take pity when he sees my fatherless children,' the mother said to herself. She took the smallest one in her arms, while the other children joined hands, and together they staggered along through the deep snow to Waldenburg Castle.

As they approached the gate they heard the sound of hunting horns and the baying of greyhounds. Suddenly the drawbridge across the moat was lowered, and a merry hunting party rode out of the castle amidst the blowing of fanfares: the whippers-in with their packs, the falconers with their birds of prey fastened to their forearms, the hunters with their spears, for that very day John of Waldenburg was minded to ride out to hunt for wild boar and hazel hens.

Those serfs who happened to be busy before the castle gate were forced to jump aside. However, the cottier's wife barred the way of the knight's horse. She sank to her knees and begged the lord of Waldenburg to release her husband. 'My lord, return their father to my children, and let them have a piece of bread, they haven't eaten since yesterday. It needn't be any larger than what you throw to your hounds — take pity, for the mercy of God, do!' She pointed to the children who were shivering with cold in their shabby clothes.

An ugly look of distaste passed across the knight's face. He called one of the whippers-in, and pointing to a big stone on the road bade him press it into the begging mother's hands.

'Here is your bread, you impudent gluttons! It is a bit hard, but at least it never goes bad. As soon as you have eaten your way through it I will release your father to show how gracious I can be!' exclaimed the knight howling with laughter till he nearly split his sides.

After such humiliation, the mother's otherwise pale face flushed with rage. She drew herself up, seized the knight's rearing horse by its harness, and yelled with all her might into the

rider's face, 'You turn to stone yourself, you monster!'

The crowd held its breath, waiting to see how the knight was going to punish the unfortunate woman. As everyone stood petrified, mouths agape, the face of John of Waldenburg began to turn grey like a rock and his eyes became glazed. His body slid down to the ground with a dull thud. A deep groan came out of his stiffening breast and a dull sound issued from his unmoving lips. Before the amazed onlookers could speak, John of Waldenburg had turned to stone.

The hunting retinue ran away in wild disorder. The horrified guests drove their horses on, galloping as far away from the castle as they could.

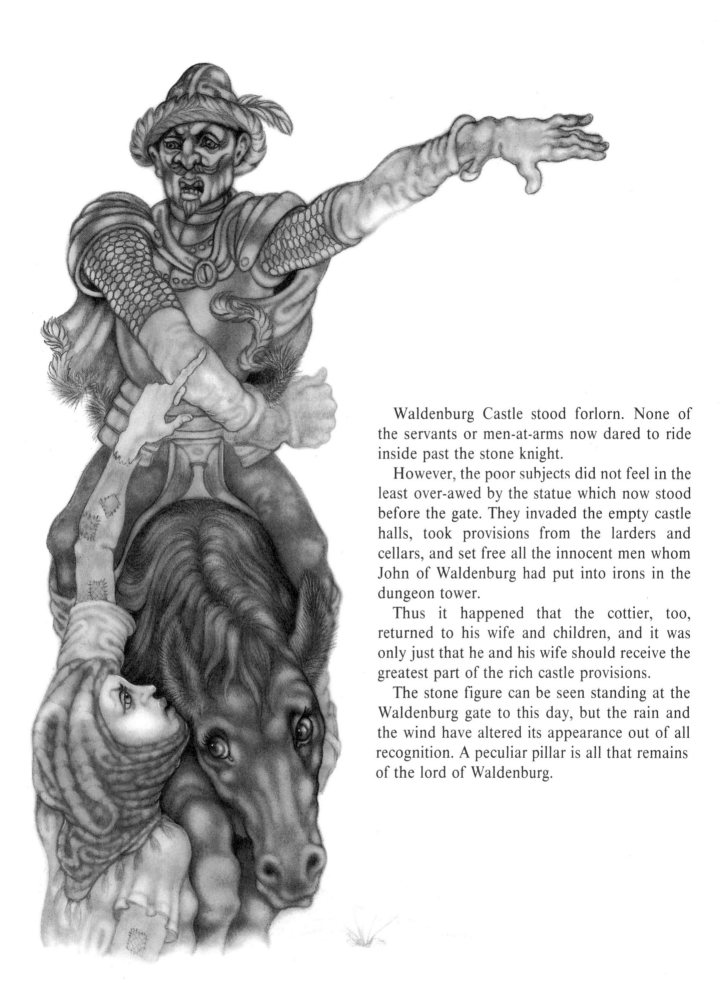

Waldenburg Castle stood forlorn. None of the servants or men-at-arms now dared to ride inside past the stone knight.

However, the poor subjects did not feel in the least over-awed by the statue which now stood before the gate. They invaded the empty castle halls, took provisions from the larders and cellars, and set free all the innocent men whom John of Waldenburg had put into irons in the dungeon tower.

Thus it happened that the cottier, too, returned to his wife and children, and it was only just that he and his wife should receive the greatest part of the rich castle provisions.

The stone figure can be seen standing at the Waldenburg gate to this day, but the rain and the wind have altered its appearance out of all recognition. A peculiar pillar is all that remains of the lord of Waldenburg.

The Wedding
at Karlštejn
Castle

During the Hussite Wars in Bohemia five hundred years ago some towns fought battles with other towns, but even more often it was castles that were besieged and captured. The famous Karlštejn Castle was no exception and one fine day Prague troops came and laid siege to it. Whoever among them believed they would take it by harvest time had to give up that hope. The Karlštejn forests and vineyards were already changing their colour to autumnal gold, the feast of Prince Wenceslas at the close of September was drawing near, and Karlštejn still held out like the rock upon which the castle was built.

Those besieged in the castle had no reason for rejoicing however, for the provisions in the castle larders were rapidly running out.

'If the Praguers do not withdraw before winter comes we shall be forced by hunger to give in,' they lamented.

The Prague troops below the castle had more pleasant thoughts to occupy their minds. They thought of how they would celebrate the St. Wenceslas feast with roasted geese.

'But it will be necessary not only to roast the festive goose, in good contentment, but also to enjoy it in peace,' cried the gourmets among them. 'Let's ask the Karlštejn people for a day's truce.'

'All right,' agreed the Prague captains, 'if only they are willing to arrange it.'

'Well, let's invite the besieged to come and feed with us,' suggested the epicures. 'Their supplies in the larders are sure to have greatly diminished after so long a siege. Let them for once grant their bellies to enjoy what they have long deserved!'

The chief soldier agreed and so did Karlštejn defenders when they got the message, for they were on the point of gnawing the bark off the oak that stood in the courtyard, their reserves had become so sadly depleted.

Thus on St. Wenceslas Day enemies became friends. Both the Prague besiegers and Karlštejn defenders were singing and feasting to their hearts' content and making friends to the point of hugging — such a glorious treat it was.

However, the guests did not forget for a moment that today would be followed by tomorrow, and the Prague troops would once again grip the castle in a stranglehold of hunger.

'It was a fair repast you prepared,' they told their Prague hosts after the meal as though praising them from sheer politeness. 'Domestic fowl is not bad, but it tastes even better when it stands on the table next to freshly fried fish, black grouse and young venison. At the castle we are used to having a choice of just what pleases the palate most, and bread and a dozen kinds of pastries, too. We've got provisions of grain and flour to last us for years,' and they took farewell in a most dignified manner.

The Praguers were dumbfounded.

'Venison! Black grouse! Fresh fish every day!' shouted a spear-carrying footsoldier who at home was an honest master of the Bakers' Guild. 'In vain are we stuck here away from our families and our shops! A fat lot of good it has done us to think we have starved out those in the castle, they have daintier food than we have!'

'Let's tear down the tents and march back to Prague this very day! The castle is sure to have some secret passage leading out into the woods and fields where the Karlštejners hunt their game,' said the hot-blooded soldiers who believed the ruse of the Karlštejn people.

Others cursed them for fools, and reproached them with wanting to clear out because they were afraid of the winter.

So quarrels arose among the besiegers. Those who had wanted to give up the siege were persuaded to hold out until the first snow appeared.

'But if the castle does not surrender by then, we will not stay a day longer. Afterwards let whoever will carry on the Karlštejn siege!' they decided.

In short, the attackers' camp was seething like an overheated cauldron. Of course, the defenders of Karlštejn were busy watching all this from the battlements, and wondering how to choose the right moment and turn the lie about the full Karlštejn larders into a truth which even the chief commander of the Prague host would give credit to.

They racked their brains until at last a solution was found.

Time passed. One day in November when the rain and wind was piercing the very bones, a parliamentary envoy set off from Karlštejn with a white flag. He begged the guards to arrange a hearing for him with the chief commander, Jan Hedvik, and having been led into his presence, bowed politely to the very ground, and said, 'On St. Wenceslas Day you asked us for a day of truce. Today we wish to ask you to grant us the same; a huntman's boy is about to marry a chamber-maid and we need a day of truce so that we can arrange a proper wedding.'

'You shall have it,' said the commander hetman graciously, and the envoy presented his compliments and made his way back.

The next day, long before noon, the soldiers from Prague heard sounds of merry music from the castle. Fiddles, pipes and drums played merry dance tunes, and the joyful shouts of the wedding guests were carried on the wind. At the same time there was not the slightest trace of a wedding at the castle. The band was playing, but nobody was dancing. Shouts greeted the bridegroom and bride of whom there was no sign either. Toasts were drunk such as are heard at rich wedding feasts but those who made them spoke above their rumbling stomachs. So skilfully did the Karlštejn folk manage to imitate in

sounds everything that belongs to a wedding feast that the Praguers who camped beyond the castle walls did not discover any ruse.

'They are rejoicing and feasting merrily up there, and down here we tremble like aspen leaves,' complained dissatisfied Prague soldiers, casting angry looks at their tents which were sodden with rain.

Up at the castle the defenders lost no time. They caught the last goat that was still running about the castle courtyard, and having slaughtered and skinned him, they separated one hind quarter and covered it with deer felt that had once served as a horse's saddle rug. In the end, the haunch looked so very much like venison that not even the King's master of the hunt discovered that it had been part of a goat.

The lord of the castle summoned a page before him, and bade him carry the haunch down to the Prague camp.

'Don't hand it over to anyone but the officer in charge, Jan Hedvik, himself,' he commanded, then instructing him word for word upon how he was to address Hedvik.

The youth was endowed with both good memory and eloquent speech. No sooner had the sentries of the attacking force taken him to the captain than he delivered his speech like an ambassador at an audience with a King, 'Your Excellency, Chief of the Prague host: The fact that you have conducted yourself in such a knightly manner today has made it possible to hold both the wedding and the wedding feast in perfect order, and all the food and drinks to be

properly consumed and digested. His Highness the royal lord of Karlštejn Castle wishes to thank you from the bottom of his heart, and so does the bridegroom himself. Here he sends a haunch from a stag brought down yesterday, with a wish that you should enjoy the rare dainty, and while doing so think of him in good spirit.'

Commander Hedvik listened to the courtly speech with great pleasure, and gave thanks for the present with equal courtesy. He nearly felt like asking the page where and how the Karlštejn people had come by the fresh venison, but in the end he preferred to dismiss him in grace and peace.

No sooner had they led the courteous youth from the camp than all those who had been standing around Hedvik and listening gathered rushed to him.

'No, we shall not capture this castle even should we lie here another five winters. We can now see with our own eyes that they have thought of everything, even secret exits and passages. Let's return to Prague, to our wives and children. We shall never starve Karlštejn out!'

Commander Hedvik looked once more at the piece of venison and bowed his head. He had to admit that his own people were right.

So it happened that on St. Martin's Day when, as it sometimes comes about in Bohemia, the first light snow dusted the woods and fields, the Prague troops ended the siege of Karlštejn and marched off empty-handed. So the defenders of the castle had cause to rejoice when they recalled how a single haunch of one old goat saved Karlštejn Castle.

The Pierced Armour at the Castle of Eltz

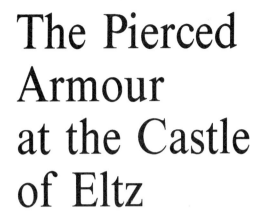

In Central Rhineland where the rivers meander gracefully between wooded hills, and the hillsides of the river valleys are overgrown with vineyards there are many picturesque castles.

The most beautiful among them is called Eltz, the same as the river which empties into the Mosele a little lower down. It looks like a fairy-tale castle: the walls of the slender towers rise steeply to noble heights crowned with a forest of turrets: the arches of the windows are bedecked with fine open-work stone tracery and numerous oriels, each one lovelier than the one before, protruding from the walls and corners.

It is obvious at first sight that the architects who built the castle did not have to stint on anything — indeed, Eltz had always been in possession of well-to-do noblemen who enjoyed respect and authority throughout the region.

One of them, as the story goes, was the father of gentle Agnes who from her earliest youth excelled in rare beauty and refinement.

At that time the neighbouring dominion was owned by the Knight of Braunsberg. He had a son only a little older than Agnes, and so the children would often play together when their parents visited each other.

'Isn't it a pleasant sight to behold?' said the lord of Eltz to the knight one day. 'Why don't we engage them to each other now? When they grow up and marry, we will become family as well.'

The lord of Eltz, let it me say, was a little scared of the noble knight of Braunsberg having heard of his passion for skirmishes and waging wars, and wondered when Braunsberg's thoughts would turn to marching against Eltz with armed power. The children's engagement would be quite sure to avert such a danger, he mused. Oh, he had no idea of how terribly mistaken he was!

The Knight of Braunsberg agreed to the proposal. In those days it was indeed a custom with noblemen to arrange their children's marriages, at a tender age. And Agnes of Eltz would be sure to receive a rich dowry, there could be no doubt about it.

The fathers were pleased with the arrangement, but nothing of the kind could be said of Agnes. The knight's son took after his father, and never tired of devising ever more roguish tricks against her. Instead of playing with her he pulled her braids, and this wasn't all; he also took great pleasure in breaking her toys, and showered her with rude insults. Later on when he grew up he treated her with even greater crudity. In the end the maiden became so disgusted with him that she avoided him wherever she could.

The young Braunsberg, however, did not mind this in the least. 'Our parents have betrothed us, and that is what counts,' he would laugh when Agnes was brought to the edge of tears by his mockery. 'As my future wife you should not scowl at me like that.'

Years passed, and the children grew up. Then, one fine day, preparations for the wedding ceremony were begun. The parents of the betrothed had invited a great company of wedding guests to the castle of Eltz: aunties, uncles,

cousins, grannies and granddads of both the families were consulting in the knightly hall how best to conduct the wedding ceremony.

The would-be bridegroom strutted up and down in front of the guests like a puffed up peacock. Agnes sat in a corner, pale and resolute, trying to gather strength. She knew that this was her last chance.

'With the eyes of all the guests turned on us I will kneel down before my parents and beg them to cancel my engagement to the Knight of Braunsberg's son. Never shall I become the wife of that ruffian even if I should have to escape from Eltz and graze cattle to earn my living,' she was musing when, all of a sudden, the bridegroom stood right in front of her.

'The relatives are making happy plans and my Agnes is scowling in a corner as though she had drunk vinegar. You had better rise, Agnes, and give me a kiss as behoves and becomes my future wife!'

'Perhaps in reward for your rudeness and your insults?' retorted Agnes, and she rose, turning her back to the bridegroom, and stepping out towards the door.

The young Braunsberg turned red in the face with rage and shame; to shame him in this way before all his relatives! Without a word he blocked the maiden's path and struck her face with his heavy riding glove.

A deathly silence fell. The entire company stood aghast at the young man's arrogance.

The first to recover was Agnes's father. He jumped at the knight's son and sent him flying from the door with such force that the young man landed upon the tiles of the corridor with a resounding thud.

At that moment all the members of the Braunsberg family rose from their seats and, mortally offended, left the hall and the castle.

From this day on the neighbours became deadly enemies. Hardly a week passed without some malicious knavery occurring between the two estates. One time the Braunsbergers released a pond full of carp belonging to the Eltzers, who in return cut out a vineyard belonging to the Braunsbergers. At other times they obstructed one another's roads with stones, drove herds into moors and crevasses, and so it went on.

In this way the little flames of ill-will were being fed more until they grew to a raging inferno and blood was shed. However, the person who delighted in all this most was Agnes's jilted bridegroom. He obtained his father's permission to command a group of selected mercenaries who undertook ever more impudent sallies against the Eltz domain in his desire for revenge upon Agnes.

'It was all your doing that I was driven from the door of Eltz Castle like a beggar, and now you shall pay dear for your rejection! My father and I will find a way to force you to say your "I will" at the altar even if it means I have to lock you up,' he whispered through clenched teeth. 'Only in this way shall I be freed from my disgrace!'

He began making plans to kidnap Agnes from Eltz. At last one day he had a feeling that he had devised the perfect ruse.

So it came to pass that some time later one of the gamekeepers in charge of the manorial border woods came running to Eltz and breathlessly reported:

'A big force of soldiers from Braunsberg Castle has marched into Badger Vale!'

Badger Vale was a rocky gorge on the border between the two manors, and only Agnes's father knew how easy it was to invade the Eltz territory from there.

'Let us lose no time,' he exclaimed on hearing the gamekeeper's news. 'We shall surround the Vale before the Braunsbergers start marching upon us!'

Leaving only a handful of his guardsmen at the castle, the lord of Eltz and all his sons set off for the remote gorge at the head of a large company of men-at-arms. He did not suspect that he had been tricked by his opponent's clever plan. Badger Gorge was empty for the treacherous gamekeeper had allowed himself to be bribed into raising a false alarm by telling a wily lie.

So the castle was left with no defence, and night was already descending on its roofs and ramparts. The young master of Braunsberg with a troop of experienced mercenaries had been waiting for some time on the opposite hillside.

'Well, haven't I played him for the fool,' he said to himself with satisfaction when he saw the lord of Eltz riding out of the gate at the head of a long cavalcade.

He remembered the mighty shove from Agnes's father that had once sent him flying from the Knights' Hall.

'Now I will have a revenge on you as well, by carrying off your beloved daughter,' he muttered under his beard, and in his mind's eyes he could see himself galloping out of the Eltz Gate with the kidnapped Agnes in his arms.

Now, of course, the castle gate was firmly secured from within with a bar, but young Braunsberg hardly found this a great impediment. From his earlier visits he knew where one could climb over the castle wall by picking out the cracks between the stones.

'Quick, before the moon rises,' he commanded the mercenaries as darkness enveloped the countryside.

The old armour-bearer who had remained as the sole guard on the outer side of the wall was sitting curled up in one of the galleries fast asleep. This enabled the intruders to climb over the rock and the wall unobserved. However, there was a surprise in store for them in the front courtyard. The second gate giving access to the palace was bolted, and that was not customary at Eltz Castle.

'Damn this wretched thing. Damn the whole devilish business!' the knight's son could not contain himself from cursing aloud. 'How shall we get inside now?'

Hearing their commander, the mercenaries would not stay behind their leader. One after the other, they started swearing outrageously, and so they woke up everyone in the castle.

Agnes was the first to rise to her feet, and looking through her chamber window out into the courtyard and seeing in the moonlight the swearing figures led by her former betrothed, she knew what was afoot. Indeed, the intruders had free access from the courtyard to the inner side of the gate. It would not be long before they pulled out the barrier beam, to use as a ram to smash the second gate which led to the palace!

'Rather than become Braunsberg's prisoner it is better to stake one's life in a fight!' thought the maiden. She ran to the armoury where her brothers' harnesses were hanging, chose the smallest belonging to the youngest one, quickly put it on, tore down the lightest of the swords from the wall, and rushed down to the Lower Hall.

The few armed men of the Eltz garrison who were left at the castle were desperately trying to work out a plan of action. Was it best to wait until the intruders broke down the gate and engage them in fighting the moment they began to pour inside, or to withdraw to one of the small turrets under the roof and trust that the door would be strong enough to stand the onslaught?

'To wait until the Braunsbergers attack with their superior numbers?' cried Agnes. 'Let us forestall their attack and come at them from the rear, that's the only way we can win through! Follow me all to the secret gate!'

The treacherous assault had awakened the maiden's courage. She donned armour and took up a sword, thereby gaining the trust of all her soldiers, from the commander to the youngest warrior. Led by Agnes they slipped out through the secret postern, and noiselessly crawled past its walls until they found themselves in the rear of the unsuspecting mercenaries.

'Down at them!' shouted the Eltz defenders all of a sudden, and attacked their confused troop with halberds, axes and hammers, anything they had been able to lay their hands on.

Agnes bore herself like a veritable comman-

der. Her armour flashed in the moonlight showing her most vulnerable point, and the Knight of Braunsberg soon became aware of this.

'So the lord of Eltz did leave his youngest son at home after all,' he said to himself when he recognized the latter's tourney harness. 'He is not doing badly considering his young age! Indeed, he is doing so well that I shall have to teach him a lesson!'

Young Braunsberg firmly gripped his heavy

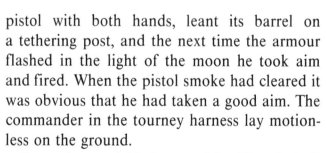

pistol with both hands, leant its barrel on a tethering post, and the next time the armour flashed in the light of the moon he took aim and fired. When the pistol smoke had cleared it was obvious that he had taken a good aim. The commander in the tourney harness lay motionless on the ground.

Braunsberg quickly leapt to him. Yes, the ball had pierced the light metal cuirass at the point where only seconds before a human heart was beating. Only then did the knight look into his victim's face, and all at once the roar of battle fell silent in his ears as he found himself staring at the dead Agnes with horror in his eyes.

He sank to his knees, pressed his forehead to the metal of the armour, and with his bare hands, began to pound the courtyard stones like a madman.

'No, this is not what I wished for, may God be my witness,' he cried again and again.

'Do not call God for witness,' a voice suddenly said behind him.

Braunsberg recognized the voice: it belonged to the old armour-bearer, Agnes's faithful guardian on all her excursions. These were the last words he ever heard, for the blow of the armour-bearer's hammer dispatched him.

Agnes's death kindled such strong feelings of revenge in the hearts of the defenders that in the darkness of the night the intruders seemed to think that the numbers of the Eltzers had suddenly trebled. The mercenaries sounded a fast retreat to the main gate — all the more so as their commander was dead. All they cared about now was to get away from the castle with as little harm to themselves as possible.

So, violence and indomitable pride had brought only death and sorrow. For a long time after this sad event visitors to Eltz Castle were shown as part of the castle collections the pierced tourney armour: the only remembrance of lovely Agnes.

The Glutton of Rodeneck

In the Tyrolean Alps castles were not built to serve the vanity of one lord above another, but to serve as defence posts for battles and wars. Many enemy expeditions had to pick their way through the Tyrolean passes and narrow river valleys if they wanted to travel from north to south or in the opposite direction. The strongly fortified castles were intended to prevent such movements.

Even Rodeneck on the narrow rocky headland above the River Rienzi, with its mighty pentagonal tower and its bastions, looked more like a fortress. The gun loopholes and oriels from which boiling pitch could be poured upon the attackers' heads awakened due respect just as the bluish grey of its stone masonry. The immense strength of the walls could only be guessed at, as could the number of crossbow shooters and blunderbusses in the roofed galleries and openings.

The spacious castle was the terror of enemies; there was no other fortress near or far to equal it. Yet not one of the owners who dwelt there in turn felt quite contented in his seat.

'Why does the outrageous spectre of Glutton lurk around the dignified halls of the castle of Rodeneck?' they would ask the chroniclers who had the history of the castle at their finger-tips. The latter only shrugged their shoulders, however, remarking: 'That was the way it has always been, ever since the castle was built.'

Glutton's residence was the labyrinth of corridors and cellars in the rock under the castle, and to try to get at him was as futile as trying to catch the wind in a net.

'Once again he has licked up all the cream from the milkjars,' complained the staff in the castle kitchen, 'and he has also been eating the apples stored up for the Christmas table!'

In fact, Glutton simply devoured everything that he came across in the cellars, and he looked like it too! Although he did his best to hide from the castle dwellers, there were some who were favoured by an accidental glimpse of him. The story they told was that the Glutton had a belly of such dimensions that he had to drive it before him on a wheel-barrow, and sitting plonk on top of it was a head as big as a pumpkin with a mouth which stretched from ear to ear. The spectre rushed through the corridors on short crooked little legs and never stopped smacking his lips, and when he opened his mouth anyone who happened to witness the sight was horrified. The food fiend's mouth was so big that it could hold a whole coach and four.

'Why has Rodeneck been chosen to bear such ills?' the equerry and captain complained as they sat down to play cards with the lord of the castle. 'We deserve a more noble spectre than one who devours cream and Christmas apples!'

'Aye, a castle of such military importance would probably be best served by a headless knight in proper harness,' suggested the captain.

'Even a skeleton rattling his white limbs would be more suitable than a pot-belly with a wheel-barrow,' added the equerry angrily.

They carried on grumbling in this way as they played cards until the lord suddenly thrust his cards on the table and said, 'We will oust Glutton with hunger! Until he is gone no respectable ghost is going to settle down here. Why, Glutton

would crunch up the headless knight even with his armour, let alone a skeleton. As from tomorrow I forbid storing cream in the cellar, even if it should turn as sour as vinegar. Likewise I will have it cleared of winter fruit.'

So, the very next day the lord's wishes were carried out, and as evening approached, Glutton kicked up such a row beneath the castle that it shook in its foundations. He created havoc like a boar gone wild, toppling shelves and stands, and even worse, with a thunderous rumbling rolled the hogsheads there and back through the corridors.

Panic-stricken, the servants sought shelter in the stables and lumber-rooms, and the equerry and lord were not laughing.

'Courage till victory is ours!' the captain of the garrison bolstered his courage as well as that of the others. 'We will starve Glutton out. He will not hold out without cream.'

As they had all hoped the spectre did vanish from the castle that very night. The first thing he came across at dawn was a turnip field not far from a nearby village. The pot-belly flung himself on the turnips like one possessed, but hardly had he plucked up and disposed of a few pieces than the peasants ran out armed with forks and flails. They took Glutton for a boar that had wreaked havoc upon their harvest with his snout and assaulted him accordingly.

Now Glutton found himself on a road leading to the town. He had had enough of the envious human breed!

However, as if just to spite him, a strange figure could be seen walking up the road towards him.

'Just the person I wanted to see, you contemptible human worm,' he mumbled gruffly, and before you could say Jack Robinson, turned himself into a guard stone.

The stone pillar was so thick that it looked more like the stump of an ancient oak, for in his true likeness Glutton was far too wide for his height.

The wayfarer turned out to be a bottle-maker. In the bedroll on his back he carried his brittle wares for sale in the town. He had already walked many miles, and when he saw a guard stone nearly as wide as a table, his face shone like a full moon.

'Here I shall relax and take a rest. At last I have something to lay my pack on!', but no sooner had he freed himself from its straps and laid the pack on the guard stone than the guard stone vanished like a dream. The pack dropped to the ground, and the bottles broke into a thou-

sand pieces. Glutton was now a myrtle-green burdock leaf. 'Why should I be a bed for some human carrying a pack?' he thought.

For a while the bottle-maker lamented over the little pile of broken bits, but instead of crying, he began to call down fire and brimstone on his ill luck, stamping angrily on the splinters and the pack.

'I'll teach you a lesson!' cried Glutton now furious, for what he could stand least of all was human screams. So he turned himself into a huge horned bullock and began to swish his tail to and fro.

The bottle-maker did not panic however; he was so enraged that he gripped the bullock by the horns, tied him with the strap of the broken pack, and ran with him head over heels to the town.

'You have appeared on the road without a master, so you are mine according to the law that holds here, and I am allowed to sell you. Indeed, that is what I shall do. At least I shall get my own back for the loss I suffered on my broken wares,' he preached to Glutton in his bullock's guise, and before the spectre had recovered from the shock, they were standing in the middle of the cattle market.

They did not have to wait long, for the strong sturdy bullock attracted the attention of a rich farmer.

'How much do you want for him?' he asked the bottle-maker.

The bottle-maker was no expert at selling cattle. He asked such a low price for the transformed Glutton that the farmer without bargaining gave the bottle-maker his asking

price, and overjoyed at the bargain led the animal away to his cow-shed.

The very first mouthful Glutton took from the heap of hay that was put into his trough by way of welcome deprived him of all hope that he would ever appease his hunger. Glutton's belly demanded what he had been used to at the castle. Dried grass was indeed a far cry from that.

'Such weeds,' snorted the gourmand through his nostrils. 'Is it for the sake of this that I am to hang around here tied to a chain?' and since he knew how to change into anything in the world, he turned into a gnat and flew out through the little window into the yard.

In the hall, the farmer's wife was just pouring cream into the butter-tub to churn it into butter. Glutton in the form of a gnat squeaked for joy and, without waiting for the farmer's wife to finish her pouring, he flew down into the churn and was at once swimming in a sea of his most favourite dainty. Before he had even managed to taste the first drop however, the farmer's wife caught him in two fingers and squeezed one of his thin gnat's legs.

'How dare that squeaky varmint now drop into my cream!' she yelled red with rage. 'Your days are numbered, you pest; I will crush you to pulp!'

Was this to be the end of Glutton? The spectre willy-nilly had no option but to return to his true likeness: that was the only way of saving his life.

The farmer's wife dropped to her knees with amazement when he appeared before her in all his width and with his wheel-barrow to boot. However, Glutton was in no mood for frightening anyone. Since the farmer's wife had squeezed his left leg it was even more crooked than before and hurt dreadfully.

He would have seen to the farmer's wife without ado, but the servants were already gathering in the courtyard crying, 'What kind of a glutton has invaded our farm?'

Before Glutton could manage to limp out of the gate they had thrown a waggon cover over him and tied him crisscross with cow's straps so that only his head showed.

'Now we've got you, you shall not escape!'

Of course, they had no inkling that Glutton knew how to get out of every tight corner.

'In a moment it will be me who will have the last laugh,' he muttered under his breath; but what he said aloud penitently was, 'I haven't had a bite since yesterday, good people. A terrible hunger is gnawing at my innards. Do what you like with me, but now I beg you for just one mouthful. A handful of soil will do!'

'Will you look at the Glutton of Rodeneck; how modest he is all of a sudden,' laughed the grooms. Glutton's fastidiousness was well known all over the place.

So they filled a whole tub of soil for him, but the moment they poured some of it into his mouth they stood dumbfounded. Glutton vanished at once as though swallowed up by the earth. When they untied the waggon cover all they found inside it was the little pile of soil which they had fed to Glutton a moment before.

They did not know that the spectre of Rodeneck would vanish without a trace if even one handful of soil were poured down his throat.

That day, Glutton disappeared from the Tyrol forever and Castle Rodeneck never again suffered under his gluttonous greed.

The Tower of the Faithful Wife

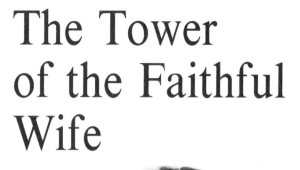

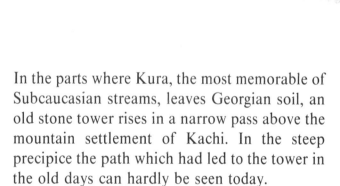

In the parts where Kura, the most memorable of Subcaucasian streams, leaves Georgian soil, an old stone tower rises in a narrow pass above the mountain settlement of Kachi. In the steep precipice the path which had led to the tower in the old days can hardly be seen today.

The story goes that the tower is the only remnant of a small castle that had once belonged to a nobleman named Torgva; he was known far and wide for his bravery and justice. He defended himself as well as the humble mountain dwellers against the ill-will of a powerful Prince who thought that Torgva's small estate did not contribute as much as it should to the Prince's treasuries.

'Are you not my vassal after all?' the Prince would ask with increasing anger each time he collected the taxes Torgva owed him. 'Don't

120

forget that the tax I have imposed on you is mine by law!'

The master of the small rocky castle was not in the habit of bowing unduly before the Prince.

'You know as well as I do, sir, that even the most well-to-do of my serfs is even worse off than the poorest farm-labourer at your court, and that even I probably have less in my pouch than any non-commissioned officer of your guard.'

'Your poverty is your own fault,' retorted the Prince. 'People say that you do not even demand a proper tithe from your serfs.'

'The little fields on the hillsides where there are more stones than soil? Is it right that I should look down from my full table on people who have nothing to eat?' Torgva replied angrily. 'My rocky castle is small, but it has always defended the whole region from the mountains to the river against foreign invasion — including your own estates, Prince! Many a mountain dweller has risked his life. Does that not seem to you a high enough tax to pay?'

So bravely did the squire answer his prince while looking straight into his eyes as his custom was.

When Torgva returned to his castle, all thoughts of the Prince's harsh words flew from his mind for there, standing at the gate to welcome him was his new young wife. He knew that his Nina was as able to defend the castle against any intruders as he himself was, so Torgva felt able to ride out without concern on long hunting expeditions into the surrounding forests.

The young couple lived together in happiness and harmony, unaware of the dark cloud gathering above them.

'That wretched vassal,' said the Prince to himself after Torgva had left. 'He talks to me as though he were my equal, and even stands up for the serfs. He opposes my will, and my patience is exhausted. I will have his rocky nest razed to the ground!'

No sooner had the Prince's thoughts turned to Torgva's small castle than his rage subsided and worry clouded his mind. He knew that the outlying field, although exposed to attacks many times had never been taken by anyone. It had but one narrow little path leading to it which was so steep that there was no other way than to climb up, mostly on all fours. A large

army would be of no use on such a difficult approach.

After thinking for a while, the Prince summoned his military commanders, men with wide fighting experience, to advise him on the best course of action. So began a heated debate; one had this idea, another that, all of them tried to expound their expertise in the art of war until all the hullabaloo gave rise to a proper row. It was only at the Prince's order that silence was restored, and then it became clear that the sentries were arguing with someone in the doorway. A man with a shepherd's staff was anxious to talk to the Prince on a matter of great importance.

'Let him in,' cried the nobleman waving his hand. As soon as the stranger approached the Prince shouted angrily, 'Well, go ahead and talk, but if your talk proves nothing but idle

chatter I will have you properly thrashed with your own staff!'

'First allow me to introduce myself, Your Grace,' the stranger stammered. 'I am the herd of your precious princely donkeys, but I won't deny that if you look upon me graciously for what I am about to tell you and reward me with a worthier office I shall not forget to be grateful to my dying day.'

'Come to the point!' cried the Prince stamping his foot impatiently, 'and no more talk of donkeys: I don't care for them.' And he thought to himself, 'I have more than enough stupid asses here in this hall.'

'I heard the great debate concerning the noble Torgva,' the fellow continued. 'I graze the donkeys by the river under his castle. You shall not bring down that vassal by power, Your Grace. His people are devoted to him heart and soul, and his seat in the rock is an impenetrable fortress. Squire Torgva can be brought to his knees only by a clever ruse. I have thought of one, with your permission.'

'Well, go on,' said the Prince and his eyes glittered with curiosity.

'At the foot of the rock,' said the shepherd, 'is a green meadow with the juiciest, most luscious grass that deer can enjoy. It's no wonder the deer from the whole neighbourhood come there to graze: only Torgva himself could say how many antlered stags he had shot in that blessed spot. He can see the pasture directly from his castle. He doesn't even have to hide in a huntsman's watch in the shrubs. If I were to adorn one of your donkeys with fine antlers and dress it in a stag's hide, and let him out properly starved on to the pasture before dawn, Torgva, the eager hunter, will not be able to resist the temptation to bring down the bogus stag.'

'Do you dare, you silly fool, to offer me a practical hunting joke with which to punish that robber?' The Prince cut the shepherd short. 'Guards, go and entertain that joker with a proper hiding!'

123

'A little more patience, Your Grace,' exclaimed the fellow, adding almost in whisper, 'If it is your desire, the joke will stop being a joke — do you wish to hear how?'

Those words rekindled the nobleman's curiosity, and he motioned to the guards to stop.

When he had finished listening to the shepherd's idea, his eyes flashed with a revengeful hope, 'It seems that a joke with such a perfect punchline is worth trying. Deck out the donkey immediately, and let him be ready this very night!'

In the twilight mist of the following morning, the lord of the castle stepped to the window, and stood in amazement at the sight before him. In the veil of mist there loomed black a crown of gigantic antlers as an eighteen-tined stag lowered them to the ground intent on grazing.

As though in a dream Torgva, the passionate hunter, seized his bow and his full quiver, and carefully descended the narrow path down to the pasture, hidden by the trunk of an ancient beech-tree, he pulled the bow-string, his hand shaking as though he were holding the bow for the first time. Never before had such a sturdy animal appeared in those parts! The shot found its target and the stag, hit by the arrow, dropped as though cut down. The hunter ran to his kill, knife drawn.

'Beware, treason, my dear!' a woman's desperate cry resounded from the castle; but too late, for at that moment Torgva fell to the ground mortally wounded by an arrow fired by an unseen hand.

Poor Nina! Too late did she see the flash of a crossbow, and Torgva fell the very moment her cry rang out.

In this way the shepherd's plan was realized

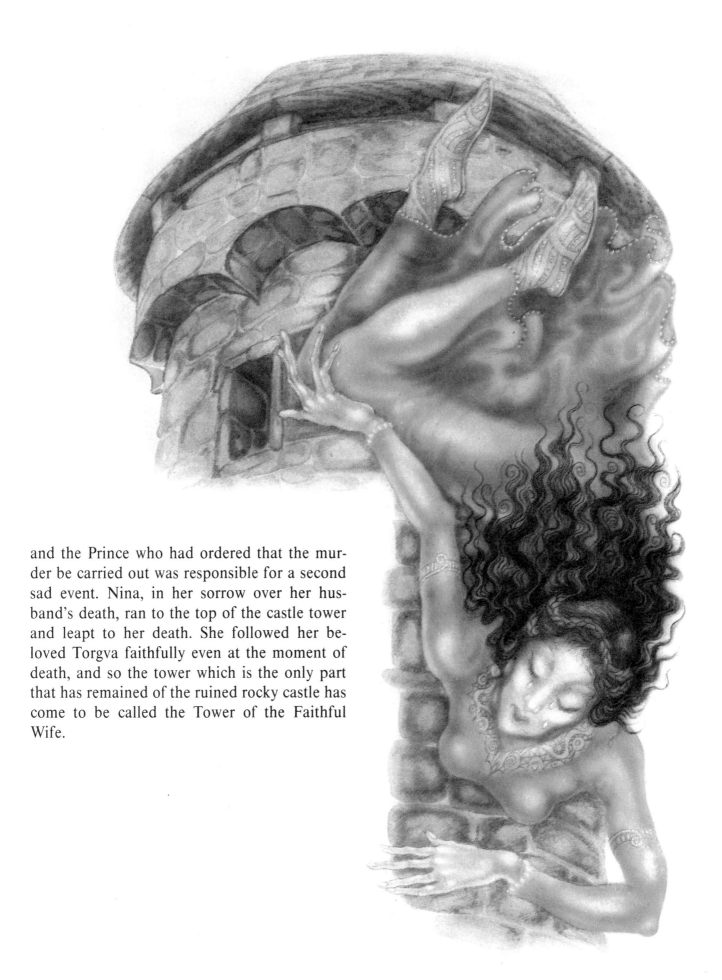

and the Prince who had ordered that the murder be carried out was responsible for a second sad event. Nina, in her sorrow over her husband's death, ran to the top of the castle tower and leapt to her death. She followed her beloved Torgva faithfully even at the moment of death, and so the tower which is the only part that has remained of the ruined rocky castle has come to be called the Tower of the Faithful Wife.

Count Dracula

Before the river Arges leaves the valley of the southern side of the Romanian Carpathians, it is just as crystal clear as high up under the snow-covered peaks of the mountain masses where it springs forth. However, there is one spot in which its waters unexpectedly turn red.

'That's a legacy from the blood of Dracula's victims,' say those who believe the ancient stories about the wooded hilltop called Poenari which towers steeply above the river. They will not accept that they are only red fragments of bricks on the riverbed that have been washed down from the ruins of Poenari Castle.

Be it as it may, blood has its place in this tale. Poenari Castle had been built centuries ago by Prince Vlad who had acquired the renown in the people's memory as having been a hard but just ruler. He would punish the guilty lord just as readily as a serf, and no thief in Walachia felt sure of himself before him — no matter how noble was the blood that ran in his veins.

While still alive he came to be nicknamed

Dracula, 'The Devil's Son', allegedly for his pitiless and cruel deeds. No one is sure how true those rumours were, and how much of it could be dismissed as slander.

Indeed, there were many who opposed him; one story held up as evidence is that of Dracula's Castle which is located above the river Arges.

The Turks were the mightiest enemies in those days. They had occupied the whole of the Balkans — why should they leave out fertile Walachia?

The local boyars, the lords of rich manors and villages, were nearly as bad as the Turks. In those hard times they should have been especially faithful to the Prince. The fact was however, that Dracula had for a long time been a thorn in their sides, for he protected the serfs from the boyar's tyranny with as much fervour as from a common thief.

One dark night the boyars gathered secretly in the city of Tirgoviste to conspire against the Prince.

'We shall bribe Dracula's servant to drop poison into the wine the Prince drinks after dinner,' whispered the first.

'And what will happen if the servant reveals this to him?' another protested.

'We should employ a murderer of our own to hide in the forest brushwood and kill the Prince with a bolt from a crossbow during a hunt,' counselled a third.

So they quarrelled with each other about how to deprive Dracula of his life until the richest boyar, the chief conspirator, put an end to all disputes:

'Your eyes are aglow with the lust for blood, and so you obviously do not see that we can kill two birds with one stone. Let us deliver Vlad to the Turkish sultan for a fat reward. He will pay in gold for such a prisoner. We shall get rid of Dracula and, in addition, make some money on it.'

Such speech found favour with all, for they were hell bent on gold. So all that remained was to devise an ingenious trap to get the Count by Easter at the latest and to get him alive. They planned to meet again in the local church to attend the Easter Mass. They parted at midnight unaware that one of them was Vlad's spy.

The moment the Count heard what was afoot he wanted to set off against the traitors and have them stuck on stakes as a warning to others.

However, when the first flames of anger had

subsided, he sat down and began to go through all he had learnt from his spy with a cool head.

'One can even learn from one's enemies,' he finally said to himself. 'For me, too, this foe may prove more useful alive than dead. We shall see!'

Easter, the greatest feast of the year, was upon them before they knew it.

The boyars put on magnificent tunics after the Hungarian fashion and used diamond buckles to fasten ostrich feathers upon their chimneys of caps. Their wives and daughters displayed rich embroideries on the silk of their luxurious skirts, and all of them wended their dignified way to church to attend the solemn mass.

The solemn hymn of the Resurrection resounded triumphantly under the roof of the cathedral, but the boyars had other things to worry about. Each of them quickly thought through all the plans, tricks and traps that he had devised against Dracula, and gloried in the thought of how much praise the other conspira-

tors were going to bestow on him during the secret session that very night.

The truth of the matter was that they had all set their hearts on how they were going to trap the Count and had no idea that it was they who were to be caught.

No sooner had the mass ended and the doors of the church opened wide than the boyars saw that they were completely encircled by Dracula's men-at-arms like deer in a hunt.

'After the festive mass on such a fine day a stroll in the mountains will not come amiss.'

It was Dracula himself who drowned the tolling of the bells in his powerful voice, and from the saddle of a sorrel as red as a flame, pointed his hammer towards the mountain tops which formed the ragged horizon high against the sky.

After this the men-at-arms rushed at the boyars and their families, using their spears to marshal them into a long procession. Before the conspirators realized what was happening, they had turned their backs on the town.

The road which led to the ancient city of Curtea de Arges, was wide and even to begin with, and the boyars took heart.

'This was only a cruel joke on Dracula's part as is his wont. He wishes to celebrate Easter in Curtea de Arges with a princely feast, and he takes care that the long walk should make us hungry,' they said.

Then, on Dracula's order they rather ran than walked through the streets of Curtea de Arges, and then the only road that led to the mountains was a narrow path full of potholes and stones. The boyar ladies complained bitterly,

for the embroidered edges of their dresses lost their splendour under a thick layer of mud. The men, however, entreated them in whisper to keep silent and not to rouse Vlad's anger. The path wound higher and higher along the river, and all that awaited them were gorges, landslides and wild beasts, hardly the stuff to feed their hope of this being a prince's whim.

The sorrel with the silent rider carried on higher and higher deep into the mountains at the head of the procession. Only on the spot where the valley of the river Arges turned into

a pass so deep and steep that the neighbouring hilltops seemed to be reaching the sky did the Count pull his horse's reins and halt.

'Can you see over there?' he pointed with his hammer to the top of a steep rock which ended above their heads in a perpendicular wall. In the giddy height there were a few half-crumbled walls silhouetted against the sky. 'That's all that is left of the castle which was once the pride of the land. You don't know that eagle's nest — you no longer even know its name, but your ancestors shed their blood on its walls, defending it against the foe. You in the luxury of your dining-halls and bed-chambers were racking your brains for a way of handing me over to the Turks for gold. Your death would be too low a price for such baseness. You shall restore your ancestors' work in order to wash the stain from their memory. From those ruins you shall build a new castle of Poenari!'

The boyars then realized that their plots had been discovered. They sank to their knees to beg Dracula's pardon. Perhaps having spared

their lives, he may be moved to even greater pity!

'We have enough serfs on our estates to complete such a construction ten times more quickly than ourselves who are unused to such labour,' they entreated. 'Indeed, we have none of us ever carried a single stone from one place to another in all our lives!'

'Enough have your serfs toiled at your own manors!' was the Count's thundering reply. 'With your own hands shall you carry the building material up to the top of the rock, and build walls so thick that they may stand up even to Turkish guns. In the rock you shall then sink a well and a corridor that will run as far as the spot where I am standing now. You shall finish the work by the feast of St. Thomas — let the sun shine on his five towers forever! Indeed, the fine white hands of your wives and daughters with whom you had plotted my ruin are sure to help you!' Having said this, Vlad turned his sorrel back and setting spurs to his sides vanished down the path like a vision.

No sooner had they fixed up some sort of shelters from wickers and branches to have some place to stay than the boyars and their wives began their work. Some hollowed out the rock with chisels and crowbars, others carried bricks and mortar on their backs, and quarried and carved the building stone. They climbed with their loads along the rock faster than the chamois, and their precious vestments were torn to rags. Even a number of boyars fell to their deaths from the smooth rocky walls into the bottomless gorges for eagles and wild animals to feed on, others at once took their places just to make sure that the castle would be ready on the day appointed.

They knew that Dracula did not jest, and that even with all the toil it was better to stay alive than to be stuck on a stake.

Thus on the feast of St. Thomas the construction was duly ready, and it shone in the morning sun like a magic castle from a fairytale.

'The masonry seems to be strong enough to withstand even the heaviest cannon balls, and the well deep enough never to dry up again. The secret passage opens far enough to allow the defenders to escape from any encirclement,' said the Count contentedly when he had inspected the entire undertaking. Then he turned to a crowd of half-naked labourers who had once been among the proudest noblemen in the land, and waved his hand saying, 'I dismiss you in grace. Return to your homes and your estates.'

'I believe I have sufficiently punished their fatuous treasons and given them enough time to grow wiser,' he said to himself, but he was yet to learn how foolish he had been.

One day when the Sultan of the Turks invaded the plains of Walachia, there was nothing left for Vlad but to retreat to the mountains. As to the boyars, they preferred to put themselves at a Turk's mercy rather than help the Count in his fight. There were but seven boyars who remained faithful to him. With these men Vlad retired in all secrecy to the castle of Poenari to make plans for their defence against the Turks.

Long were the deliberations around the oak table in the knight's hall. With darkness already descending they could barely see each other, so they lit a single candle not to give themselves away by having the windows lit too brightly.

Suddenly a loud crash resounded and the company leapt from their seats as one man: an arrow shot from outside had pierced the window pane and landed straight on the table among them. At that moment a cold breath of air blew into the hall and extinguished the candle. When they succeeded in relighting it, they found a note firmly tied to the arrow with a horsehair.

The faithful boyars looked at each other with an ominous sense of foreboding. What kind of news could such a note bring?

Already the Count had impatiently broken the horsehair and spreading the roll read aloud:

'Vlad, You Most Gracious Prince!

The Turks are near — nearer than you suspect. They had got as far as here to Pietraria. Had even dragged up their guns to the mountain top and want to destroy your castle with a hail of shots. It is best that you all flee from there while the exit is still free!'

Pietraria was the mountain that towered right beside the rock with the castle of Poenari on it that could easily be fired upon from there.

'I do recognize the handwriting,' sighed the Count when he had done reading. 'It belongs to my nephew whom the Sultan captured and has been dragging around all his camps as a hostage. Lo and behold, even the Sultan himself has deigned to take pains to climb up to Pietraria! My sister's son's warning is well-meant. He does not believe in the strength of the walls and towers of Poenari, but then he has never seen them from inside! At my instruction the boyars have built them twice as strong as usual, and I should like to see the gun that could do damage to them.'

To hold out in the castle until the Turks exhausted with the vain siege would retire! Such was Vlad's will and none of his faithful allies had a mind to oppose it.

With the break of dawn, the Turks began to fire from all their guns as though it were a shooting contest. Count Vlad could only look on in amazement as in the rain of the cannon balls the ramparts crumbled like cake and the walls of the tower fell apart like crock.

It was a clever revenge the boyars had taken for the bloody toil during the building of Poena-

ri: instead of mortar they had used thin clay to hold the bricks and stones together, and the walls they built were only strong to look at; inside they were hollow and thin like a shell.

'Oh, God, I wish I had had those treacherous men impaled after all!' raged the Count. 'From this day on I shall never be able to get enough human blood!'

Nor were the Turks spared a fateful disappointment. When they were bombarding the castle for the third day in succession, they decided it was time to take its remnants by storm. Like dogs on all fours they were forced to climb up the steep rocks and many of them like the toiling boyars before them found their death in the abysmal depths.

However, to break into the castle up above was far easier than they could have imagined for not a living soul opposed them. All inside was quiet: there was no trace of Dracula or his retinue. So they marched empty-handed back to the mountains from whence they had come.

The story passed amongst the populace that Count Vlad with his faithful few had escaped by a secret passage to the river Arges, and travelling upstream reached safety as far away as in Transylvania on the other side of the Carpathian range.

Then there were others who claimed that transformed by his own curse into a vampire, he hid in a coffin in a certain remote chamber of the Poenari ruin. On moonlit nights, when the eerie howl of wolves resounds from the neighbouring woods, they say there is still a pale light flickering behind the openings of the windows in what is left of the castle wall. It is Dracula rising from the coffin in which, neither alive nor dead, he sleeps by day, and candlestick in hand, plans his wicked deeds. He unfolds the webbed fans of his bat's wings that grow anew night after night, and leaves the castle in silent flight to satiate himself with human blood. Before daybreak he returns to the castle ruins.

He who is able to find Dracula sleeping in his

horrible bed can rid mankind and Dracula himself from this terrible curse. However, it is only the bravest among mankind who would have the courage to perform such a task for he must pierce the Count's heart with a wooden stake of the kind upon which he himself would have condemned men impaled during the time of reign.

This is the only way Dracula, or Vlad the Impaler as he is also known, can really die and thereby gain eternal peace. There is no other way.

The Enchanted Castle in the Olsztyn Forest

In the north of Poland, in the Mazuria region where there are thousands of lakes, a forest castle is said to have stood in olden days near the town of Olsztyn. On one of the hills above the river Lyna wood-cutters often came upon oblique slabs overgrown with moss and grass, which looked like the roof of a large construction which had sunk down into the earth. They say shepherd lads would throw pebbles into the mysterious openings between the slabs and listen to how they clattered deep down inside as though falling down a long shaft.

Today everything has become overgrown with thorns and brambles and all that remains is an ancient legend from the days of yore.

The lord of the forest castle was one of the richest nobles in the land: it was rumoured that there were about as many as a hundred coffers of gold, silver and precious stones in his treasury. Rare tapestries hung upon the walls of the castle chambers and halls, and the floors were covered with the furs of giant bears and wolves with which the neighbouring woods teemed.

However, the most magnificent ornamentation was to be found in the knightly hall: its walls were from top to bottom inlaid with amber, the gold and yellow jewel of the North. It was to this chamber that the subjects would come to air their wishes and grievances, and they would all be kindly received and justly dealt with. For the lord of the castle was a nobleman equally good as he was rich: he looked after his people like a good husbandman: there was not a man on his estate who would suffer from want.

The master was husbandman to his people and Warmia, his spouse, was a kind and gentle mother to them. She treated the sick ones, and helped those who suffered from some wrong as though they were her own children. For it was with love that she had brought up her own twelve sons as well: as they grew up each of them at his own redoubt or stronghold helped in building up their father's wide dominion.

Once a year they all gathered at their native castle near Olsztyn with their wives and children. Lady Warmia side by side with her husband would welcome the guests in her white Sunday attire girded with a ribbon as red as the flower of the poppy and a fine veil covering her silver-grey hair. She caressed her grandchildren, and then the whole castle echoed with joy over the unusual meeting. The adjoining woods echoed with tally-hos of hunting parties, and the banqueting hall resounded with unending talk and laughter. There were, indeed, many things to talk about, for they had not seen one another for a whole long year.

A week later they all drove back to their respective homes, and the castle near Olsztyn was once again submerged in the silence of the deep forests.

To everybody's delight such was the scene on Midsummer Day year after year, until one summer, when the castle was all abustle with preparations for the family feast, an exhausted rider reported to the castle gate. He was Squire Leshek, an old friend of the lord of the castle, and he had just returned from his journeyings.

'It is not good news that I bring you, dear brother,' he exclaimed when he was ushered into the lord's chamber. 'Things are so bad that I did not even stop at my own home, but have hurried to you without any delay. Two of the most powerful chieftains in the neighbourhood are mustering a big army. I saw it with my own eyes! They are out to conquer your domain and to wreck your castle. They loathe the way you look after the welfare of your subjects, and the

the castle great concern and he ordered that a fire be made at the highest bastion. This was an agreed signal for his sons to come to his aid with their men-at-arms as quickly as possible.

It was by a hair's breadth that they arrived at their father's dominion in time; the enemy had already invaded the estate, and were rapidly advancing towards the forest castle. Even before dark the defenders on the walls were able to see smoke rising from the woods all around.

'They have pitched camp already, and they seem to be great enough in number to overthrow us!' said the lord of the castle dismally, embracing his wife who had turned pale with fear.

'The castle will not stand up to such overwhelming odds. The only thing that may save us from death and ruin is the magic of this Midsummer Night,' she replied.

At that very moment a very anxious little boy whose name was John ran out of a cottage on the opposite side of the forest. His mother had fallen ill suddenly, and he was the only other person in the house. His father was no longer alive; he had died whilst felling an ancient oak tree.

The boy ran to the castle for all he was worth. 'The good lady Warmia is sure to give me some medicine to make Mother well again!' he said to himself and ran even faster.

On that Midsummer Night the stars in the sky sparkled even more brightly than usual, and the light of the full moon veiled the tree-tops in silver garb. Was it only the moonlight glimmering on the branches, or was it some magic that had made a path on the darkened moss of the forest floor? The boy set off as though in a dream, and the path led him to places never before visited by man.

Suddenly, a mysterious light appeared somewhere ahead of him. As he approached it he saw that the path ended in a clearing in the middle of which there grew the mightiest cluster of bracken the boy had ever seen. There was

kindness of your wife to the sick and the orphans has been a thorn in their side. They fear that their people might demand the same!'

The lord of the castle cast a sad look over the keep with its arrow slits overgrown with ivy, at the walls hidden under flowing cascades of bright flowers, at the bastions from which not the barrels of guns, but green brushwood stuck out.

'In my lifetime not a single shot has been fired from this castle, not a single weapon has been wielded,' he said with a sigh. 'Why should it have been otherwise? The borders of my dominion have never been crossed by the foot of any aggressor.'

'But now the neighbourhood is teeming with them, dear friend. Don't delay: strengthen the castle's defences,' Squire Leshek urged the lord.

His voice was so stern as to cause the lord of

a flower swinging on its silvery stem whose calix and petals shone with pure gold!

Little John, who knew every forest plant and every tree, gasped in amazement. He had never seen such beauty in his life.

'Come and pluck me,' a tender bell-like voice invited.

John tiptoed to the stem, and the moment he touched it the flower seemed to skip into his fingers, so easy was it to pluck.

'I will give it to Lady Warmia, she is sure to like it,' said the boy to himself, and ran on. He nearly forgot all about his mother lying ill at home.

The flower shone like a lantern lighting the way for him, but the boy had no idea of the magic power it contained, for unknown to himself, he became invisible, nor was he able to see the attacking soldiers. Before long he had passed unobserved and unopposed through the enemy camps which surrounded the castle on all sides.

He knew nothing of the danger threatening the forest castle, and so when he reached the gate he gaped with astonishment for the oak railings had been lowered, barring the way. As far as John could remember this had never happened before. He often used to visit Lady Warmia, bringing her baskets of the first wood strawberries and raspberries out of gratitude for her kindness.

To his amazement he saw the gate open of its own accord to such a height as to allow him to slip inside, and dropped back at once behind him.

Although the hour was late, the castle was all

astir. Every hand turned to carrying their meagre supplies of ammunition from the armoury up to the bastions and galleries, and the garrison men-at-arms were running to man their posts in the keeps and on the battlements.

John, who had no inkling of the encirclement, did not know what was afoot. When he saw the brightly lit palace windows he started running to the staircase where Lady Warmia would welcome him whenever he came. Now she stood there pale and grave by her husband's side. In the vestibule of the Amber Hall they were talking to the garrison commander and wondering whether there may be a glimmer of hope after all that the castle would withstand the bitter attackers.

'Even if we should withstand their assaults, they will starve us out,' said the lord of the castle bowing his head. Overwhelming forces have laid siege to the castle. 'Woe to my people when it falls into the enemy's hands!'

Meanwhile, John ran up the staircase and thrust into Lady Warmia's hand the miraculous bracken flower.

'I have brought you a flower for joy, do not be sad any more, dear lady.'

With tears in her eyes she pressed him to her heart. The golden flower of bracken! In her youth she had heard tell of it, for it blooms but once in a year on Midsummer Night, and whoever may find it, to him it will open every way according to his will and desire.

When John told Lady Warmia about his mother's illness, she gave him a mixture of the rarest herbs from her medicine chest, and led the boy to a secret underground passage.

'This tunnel will lead you to the other side of the forest, John, not far from where your little cottage stands. In some places the walls caved in having been washed away by an underground stream. A grown man could not pass through those openings but you are small and thin, you will get through unscathed. You cannot travel through the forest, we are encircled by enemies. When your mother recovers seek out good people and tell them all they should not despair. Our army may have to go to sleep now under the earth and stay there for centuries; but a day will come when it will wake and bring freedom to the land. Let them pass on that message from generation to generation!'

In parting, Lady Warmia pressed a motherly kiss on John's cheek, and returned to her husband.

As they were entering the Amber Hall together, she held above her the golden flower, and it happened that the castle's soldiers began to form ranks behind its blaze as they would behind a battle banner. Only then when one began to take his place beside the other in the Amber Hall could one see what a numerous host it really was.

The lady encompassed them all with a kind smile, lowered her arm, and turned the shining gold flower towards the ground. At that moment a silvery note sounded in the hall, high and all-pervading which seemed to make even the thick castle walls tremble. Those who stood by the windows witnessed an unbelievable sight: the dark horizon of the forests against the fading pre-dawn sky began to ascend to the sky as if thousands of its trunks were suddenly growing up into the heights with magic speed.

This was only an illusion, however, for in reality the forest castle began sinking lower and lower and was slowly descending underground with all its towers, gates and bastions. The gold bracken flower had become a magic key in Warmia's hands and an abyss had opened beneath the castle growing ever deeper and deeper into the bowels of the Earth.

As the castle disappeared beneath the ground the numbers of men-at-arms in the Amber Hall grew apace, with no one knowing where they were coming from. Before even the roof of the Palace sank into the ground, they had filled the entire hall and its adjoining corridors to overflowing. Rattling their armour they were tread-

ing the wooden stairs up into the refuge tower, and running down into the underground caves.

When the last vane and the tip of the tallest tower had disappeared beneath the soil and the whole of the forest castle had vanished without a trace into its depths, it was full to the last recess of soldiers armed to the teeth.

The tale was passed from generation to generation of the great army which slept silently in the underground castle, and that it would awaken when the time came.

Only a figure wrapped in a white veil is said to wander in the parts where the castle had once stood along the gold-glittering waves of the River Lyna. It is Lady Warmia who unlocks the Earth with the magic flower of bracken and comes up into the world to remind new generations of the ancient message.

The Enchanted Ermesinda

In Luxemburg on the hills called Johannisberg and Zolverknapp and in a place bearing the name of Hesperingen, there are three castle ruins standing to this very day. In the times of their greatest renown the castles belonged to a nobleman who had three sons. When the father died, the brothers divided the whole dominion into three equal parts, and made a solemn pledge of mutual trust and alliance. If any one of them were to be threatened with danger, the other two would be bound to run to his aid with their men-at-arms.

Soon after that the eldest son, who inherited Johannisberg from his father, got married. He had brought home a bride from a noble Burgundian family, and when after a time a little daughter called Ermesinda was born to them, she was both loved and adored by the whole family.

'Look at that noble forehead above her charming little face!' the happy father would say to his frequent visitors.

'Indeed, she brings no dishonour on the noble family from which she springs,' her uncles and aunts vied in glorifying her, and showered the rarest gifts on Ermesinda from the very cradle.

Matters reached their climax when Ermesinda grew up into a real beauty who found no equal in the whole of Luxemburg. The flattering of aunts, uncles and cousins knew no bounds. Knowledge of Ermesinda spread through the land and although it seems hard to believe, both of her uncles bequeathed their castles on Zolverknapp and at Hesperingen together with their estates to their niece Ermesinda! They were said to have declared that they would rather never marry so as to be sure that Ermesinda should become their heir.

Everyone was astounded at the unheard of generosity — only Ermesinda looked as though nothing could be more normal. She had become so used to being pampered and admired that even if the ruler of India himself were to place all the treasures of his empire at her feet she would not be surprised.

She became more conceited and more avaricious the more praise and gifts were bestowed upon her. The time came for her to marry, and suitors came prowling around Johannisberg. The unmarried sons of noblemen came from far and near to pay tribute to the beauty of Johannisberg and bring her all manner of gifts.

However, Ermesinda only led them up the garden path. She would say to one that she may really fall in love with him one day, and to an-other that she could not imagine anyone better as her husband than him, and to a third that he should just go on wooing her, and bringing ever more beautiful presents, for patience conquers the world. Thus putting an innocent face on it all, she let herself be courted by a host of suitors, and only derided them all in her heart of hearts. She already had treasuries full of gold and jewels and thought nothing of running her fingers through them all day long. Even her favourite black poodle who never left her side would sniff at every bracelet and every ring.

Ermesinda's father and mother were not at all happy with the way things had turned out for they now realized that all the pampering and pandering which the whole family had showered upon her from her earliest days had turned

their daughter into a spoiled heartless niggard.

'It is not right for a maiden of a good family to trifle so fancifully with her suitors,' her parents would scold, but Ermesinda would only laugh and say:

'Am I to compliment them? I don't care for a single one of those milksops so that's that!'

Word of Ermesinda's beauty reached the ears of a particular young Count of Luxemburg. He was the only descendant of a worthy old family, and was just about to take up the rule over his domains. For some time past he had been looking for a suitable bride, and so he now decided to ride to Johannisberg to court the spoilt maiden.

He was captivated by her beauty at first sight and without hesitation asked Ermesinda if she thought she could become his wife.

'Well, why not, anything could happen,' she answered with a charming smile, for this was the kind of answer she gave to all her suitors.

However, the Count of Luxemburg took Ermesinda's reply for a consent, and asked her parents for her hand.

Of course, they did not refuse for the Luxemburg family was the most highly esteemed in the whole country and they also lived in hope that such a noble marriage may one day make Ermesinda mend her ways. Preparations for the wedding began immediately.

Guests began to arrive at Johannisberg long before the wedding day. The otherwise quiet castle suddenly resounded with feasting, the hubbub of tourney joustings and tally-hos from the adjoining forests.

'What is all this hustle and bustle about? The castle is boiling like an overheated kettle!' Ermesinda asked her father angrily after a few days. 'I do not even have enough peace and quiet to try on my new dresses and jewels!'

'Have patience, dear daughter, just a little patience. Don't you think your marriage to the Count of Luxemburg deserves this festive mood?' replied the lord of Johannisberg with

a kind smile, thinking that Ermesinda was anxious to be married.

'The Count of Luxemburg? But I had forgotten all about him long ago, dear father! Think how many suitors have passed through this place! Who could remember them all?'

The father was thunderstruck by his daughter's reply. He then became consumed with rage, and ended his tirade by threatening Ermesinda that he would have her shut up in a nunnery unless she grew wise and changed her mind.

'You shall see she will eventually decide for the best,' said the Lady of Johannisberg trying to allay her husband's anger, and from that moment on she never stopped trying to persuade her daughter to give up her pig-headed defiance and be mindful of the honour of her family.

However, the proud Ermesinda's answers to her mother were never the same for she changed her mind like the wind. When her mother entreated her daughter with tears in her eyes, the maiden dismissed her wishes saying, 'Oh, mother, I am getting tired of all this. Leave me in peace until the wedding day. We shall see, but now do go away, please do!'

'Perhaps she will do as she is told in the end,' thought her mother and went away hoping her daughter would come to her senses yet.

The Count of Luxemburg arrived at the castle on the eve of the wedding. On the tower galleries of Johannisberg festive camp fires flared, and amidst the sound of tolling bells youths and maidens from the settlement around the castle gathered in the Johannisberg chapel. According to old custom they were to hand a wedding nosegay of the loveliest meadow flowers to the bride to be.

The chapel buzzed with anticipation. The bridegroom, the bride's parents and relatives had been in their places for some time, but the one upon whose account they had all gathered together was not there.

The murmur slowly died down, and an oppressive silence spread throughout the chapel. The guests started giving each other anxious glances and the bridegroom's fingers drummed impatiently upon the hilt of his sword. The Lord of Johannisberg stared glumly at the stone floor of the chapel, unsure of what to do.

No one noticed Ermesinda's mother slipping out of the chapel and hastening to her daughter's chamber.

'She may have been delayed with her dressing as she sometimes is,' she thought hopefully, but in truth, a different picture presented itself when she reached the maiden's room.

Ermesinda was sitting in her chamber in a state of half-undress, her black poodle at her feet. She sat in front of the looking glass, lazily combing her raven hair.

'I have changed my mind,' she announced still looking at her reflection in the mirror. Her mother was so terrified that she could not utter a single word. 'I am not going to get married tomorrow after all. Tell Father if you will that I am as little interested in the Count of Luxemburg as in all the others before him!'

'May the earth swallow you up along with all your gold and treasuries!' yelled the Lady of Johannisberg and ran out of the chamber as though she had lost all her senses.

Suddenly there was a terrific explosion, which caused her to turn in the doorway. In the spot where Ermesinda once sat, a large black hole had opened up and from it rose huge clouds of a sulphurous smoke. The curse was fulfilled!

The terrified woman ran back to the chapel to tell her husband the ghastly news, but she saw him, together with the others, out in the courtyard which was lit up by the light of a raging

fire. The explosion had been so powerful that it shook even the main tower, and burning logs from the festive camp fires showered down from the galleries. The whole castle appeared to be alight!

'My curse has made Ermesinda perish! May the earth swallow me up as well,' cried the desperate mother, throwing herself to the ground.

The Lord of Johannisberg looked at the lady

who lay at his feet, her eyes now deranged with sorrow. In great shame he drew a gold dagger and thrust it into his breast, and thus sank dead into the arms of his Hesperingen brother who was standing at his side. Nor was this, alas, to be the last death at the hapless Johannisberg Castle! The lord's other brother, the owner of the residence at Zolverknapp, leapt to the side of Ermesinda's mother, and in a fit of sudden hatred stabbed her with his sword.

'You too perish, you are the cause of the whole misfortune!' he shouted like a madman.

In great dismay the wedding guests sprang to their steeds to flee from the scene of destruction, and with them, his face full of horror, the Count of Luxemburg himself.

The next morning all that was left of the once imposing Johannisberg Castle, was a smoking ruin, but even this was to be smashed to pieces and pulled down at the behest of the surviving brothers.

'Let nothing but a pile of stones mark that hill of damnation and bloody deeds!'

These were the last words that anyone in the country ever heard the brothers speak. Early one morning they left their castles in the horsehair garb of penitents on a pilgrimage to the Holy Land, never to return again.

Since those days a tale has been told in the lands which lie in the shadow of Johannisberg Hill, about the enchanted Wild Maiden.

On dark, stormy nights she is said to ride out in a fiery carriage without horses across fields and forests. The wheels of the carriage float above the earth like ravens flying. One moment the Wild Maiden sits on the driver's box, the next inside again combing her raven hair as on that day long long ago when she was cursed by

her own mother before the looking glass in her castle chamber.

Yes, it is indeed the lovely Ermesinda. After the ride she vanishes again along with the carriage inside Johannisberg Hill where coffers overflowing with gold and jewels await her. She is said to be sorting through the gifts of her suitors now long dead, and again and again contemplating one jewel after another, with the shaggy black poodle running about her legs like a faithful guard. Once a year, on the anniversary of the curse, Ermesinda's dog runs out of the hill, and appears before people with a big key in his mouth. Whoever is able to gain possession of the key will win the maiden for his bride, together with all her treasures.

There have been many who have dared to try, but as soon as they wanted to touch the key, it turned white with heat, and the poodle became a fiery monster belching forth flames, stinking smoke billowing from its nostrils.

So there sits the beautiful Ermesinda buried beneath the earth, amidst her coffers, and waiting to be disenchanted from her mother's curse.

How the Blacksmith of Fumel Made the Princess Laugh

Before Henry IV, King of Navarre, became king of all France he dwelt with the greatest of pleasure at the castle of Nérac in his own dear Gascony. The castle walls and windows were decorated with rows of fine pillars and the banqueting hall even boasted a treble fireplace. However, even a King's life is not all roses: there were days when Henry IV would gaze into the flames and feel most disconsolate.

'People say I am rich, generous, just and as brave as a lion,' he mused. 'But in real fact I am a most unhappy man. My only daughter will not give a smile all the year round; no wonder she is called Little Sad-Face. My stables are replete with horses, but they are all coal black. I am fond of my lovely great white and would fain ride him every day racing with the wind. Only the white will not let himself be shod; not even the handiest smith in the neighbourhood can make him stand still and shoe him. Not in vain has he been dubbed Break-Iron, Break-Shoe and God knows how many other names. Indeed, I am the most miserable of all kings, and this must be put an end to.'

So one day Henry IV called his town crier and drummer to his presence, and pushing a pouch of pistoles into his hand said, 'Get

At that time there was a young blacksmith plying his trade in the township of Fumel, about two days' journey from Nérac. He feared no one, not even the devil himself; so why should he be afraid of the sad Princess or of the Break-Iron horse even if the white had never stood still for any blacksmith to shoe him?

When the master of the black trade heard the King's announcement he put into his leather bag four of the strongest horseshoes that he found in his stock and for each horseshoe, seven twice-forged nails, and adding to them a hammer, a loaf of bread and a flask of wine he set out in the direction of the township and castle of Nérac.

As he trudged along he suddenly became very hungry and thirsty. So he sat down by the roadside, cut one slice of bread after the other and washed them down with wine. Suddenly, he could hear a cricket in a nearby field of wheat. This was no ordinary cricket, for he knew the speech of men and asked the blacksmith without ado where he was going.

'To Nérac Castle to see the King,' answered the blacksmith. 'If I make Princess Sad-Face laugh and get Break-Shoe horse shod I shall become the King's son-in-law and shall inherit the crown.'

'To see the King you say? And would you not take me with you? I, too, would be delighted to see our good old King. Perhaps one day I can return your kindness, what do you think?'

The blacksmith was fond of crickets, for they used to cheer him up with their song back home in his smithy.

'Of course, I will, with pleasure. Just jump into my beard.' The cricket hopped up and the next moment he was swinging on the blacksmith's chin.

So they set out on their journey. The blacksmith strode out to the cricket's song until the man's stomach was rumbling with hunger once again. So he sat down at the edge of a field as before. Only that field had no wheat growing in

ready to set out into the world, drummer, and wherever you come to you are to drum up people and proclaim that he who succeeds in making my daughter laugh and in shoeing my horse shall have the Princess's hand in marriage and become my heir.'

So the drummer set about announcing the King's proclamation in every village and market town. Before long Nérac Castle simply teemed with wooers, but none of them had any luck either with the Princess or with the white. So they just had to go back from whence they came empty-handed.

it. It was a tobacco field and he saw a little mouse relishing some of its leaves.

Strangely enough, she too knew human speech, and just as the cricket before her wished to go to Nérac and look at the King.

'You may find it useful if I render you a little service,' she said to the blacksmith.

'Of course, you may come, with pleasure,' said the blacksmith and told the little mouse to climb up on to his beret.

Even the flea that bit the blacksmith's nose when he put up for the night at an inn in the town of Agen spoke the way the humans do, and desired to see the King whose name was Henry.

'I am not a nobody, you know. I am the Queen of the Fleas,' she declared. 'I can give you valuable help if you take me with you.'

'Why of course, I will. With pleasure,' replied the blacksmith. 'Since you have bitten me in the nose you may as well stay there. Just make sure you hold on to it firmly enough.'

So the next day all the four of them appeared at Nérac, and happened to cross the path of the Princess as she was returning from a walk before dinner with her royal father.

When the Princess saw the mouse squatting on the blacksmith's beret, the corners of her mouth twitched. When she heard the cricket chirping from the man's beard, a smile flitted on her lips, and when she saw the flea dancing on the tip of the traveller's nose, the King's

daughter burst into such a fit of laughter that she was nearly gasping for breath.

'So that disposes of a half of my job,' said the blacksmith presenting his compliments at the feet of that noble couple. 'You know, Your Majesty, I have come to make merry your daughter Sad-Face who had never before given a laugh, and to shoe your horse Break-Shoe who has never let himself be shod by anyone,' he added by way of explanation.

'You are right, young man,' said the King. 'The Princess has begun to laugh, there is no denying that. But now off to the Court and to the stable of my white.'

The moment the horse who was known as Break-Iron saw the blacksmith pull the horse-shoes, the nails and the hammer out of his bag, he started prancing upon all fours, snorting and neighing till the sounds he made could be heard seven miles away.

The blacksmith thrust his hand into his beard and said, 'Well, cricket, won't you set to work now?' and that very moment the cricket jumped off the blacksmith's chin straight into the horse's ear and started such a twitter that Break-Iron turned quite deaf. He bent his head down to the ground and became as gentle as a lamb.

'This is where you come in, mouse,' said the blacksmith stretching his arm to his beret, and with one single jump the mouse landed close to the white's nostrils and blew away with such abandon that Break-Iron turned over to one side and sank into a deep sleep.

You see, the mouse had been feeding on to-bacco leaves, she found them simply delicious, and her breath was full of the drug, and Break-Iron was not accustomed to it. In those days tobacco was still accounted a great rarity in France.

Thus the blacksmith was able to set to work unhindered, and he had the white shod before you could say Jack Robinson.

'Now I am ready,' he laughed presenting his

work to the monarch. 'Well, it might be so,' admitted the King, but then he leant towards the blacksmith and whispered into his ear, 'You are still at liberty to change your mind. You will not have an easy life of it with my daughter. She is spoilt and can make a man's life a misery. What about exchanging the marriage for a fine round pouch of Spanish gold quadruples? Just think: even one quadruple is no negligible sum. One quadruple amounts to four gold pistoles, and that is great deal of money.'

The blacksmith was silent for a while and then said, 'Well, I agree. But nevertheless I shall regret not marrying the Princess whom I got laughing. May I at least come to the church on her wedding day?'

'That you can do even today, blacksmith,' said the King with a smile. 'There has been a very noble suitor waiting in the inn beneath the castle for a whole month now. All he is waiting for is my permission. At long last I am in the position to give it to him, since my daughter is the Sad Princess no longer.'

A King can do anything. It is no trouble for a King to arrange his daughter's wedding in two hours: a mere trifle for a crowned head.

The bridegroom was their greatest trouble: though a Duke with a domain nearly so large as the King's he just could not press his belly into his best pair of trousers!

At long last the bride and the bridegroom knelt down before the altar at the Nérac church,

and the blacksmith who had found himself a seat in the first pew right behind the bridegroom quickly put his hand to his nose. Hop! And lo, the flea in a marvellous curve landed behind the bridegroom's neck. Once there she did nothing but bite, tickle, race and skip to and fro, from the Duke's scruff she slipped down under his shirt playing the devil until he could bear it no longer.

Only for a few moments did the bridegroom fidget and scratch, but wedding or no wedding, he jumped up nearly knocking down the reverend parson. Now he was wheeling around, the next moment he was jumping up and down on one foot.

'He must be possessed,' cried the parson taking refuge in the vestry. In the end, amidst great uproar and confusion, the bailiffs bound the 'possessed' man hand and foot and carried him out of the church.

'I do not want a bridegroom who does not know how to behave even when he is at church!' the Princess cried. 'I would much rather marry that blacksmith of Fumel, at least he knows how to make a body laugh.'

What was the King to do? He had no other choice but to agree.

So in the end the blacksmith of Fumel did become the King's son-in-law and heir to the throne, as was solemnly laid down, signed, and certified at the ancient Castle of Nérac in the region called Gascony.

How Wemyss O'Logie Fled from the Dungeon of Edinburgh Castle

It happened in the days when James the Sixth was still reigning in Scotland that on a winter night his faithful old footman departed to his last resting place. In those eventful times it was far from easy to find a reliable successor; in the end, the King decided in favour of a poor squire's son, the young Wemyss O'Logie, who thus became a new footman at the royal castle of Edinburgh.

However, before long the proud Scotsman found it extremely irksome that the King drove him relentlessly from morning till night.

The gloom in the young man's spirits lifted only when he chanced upon the kindly red-haired Margaret. She was the Queen's Danish chambermaid, with a radiant smile. They were able to exchange only a few words each time they happened to meet in the course of their duties about the place: neither the King nor the Queen allowed their servants to idle their time away. However, even those brief meetings were enough for them to fall in love with each other. This did not lessen Wemyss's dissatisfaction with his occupation however; rather the opposite in fact.

Whenever he could he would wander off to an out-of-the-way inn to drown his sorrows and forget the humiliation the King brought to bear upon him from morning to night. However, instead of enjoying the draught, Wemyss could only clench his fists and scowl in anger. What was worse, having consumed one or two jugs over his limit, he took to muttering insults and curses that could only have been meant for his lord and master.

As though decreed by Fate itself, there was another great plot brewing against the monarch at the very same time. It was led by the Earl of Bothwell whose family had hated King James from his infant days.

The conspirators agreed the best thing to do would be secretly to enter the King's chamber at night and take him captive while still in his bed. It was no trouble at all to find out that the King's peaceful sleep was being safeguarded by a single servant: the young O'Logie whose duty it was to sleep each night in the anteroom of the King's bedchamber and to lock it up with a key which was solely in his possession.

The conspirators planned to try to win over the squire's son as an ally, but the question was how was this to be achieved? Bothwell was well aware that no O'Logie had ever allowed himself to be bribed, no matter how poor he was, and so he nearly whooped with joy when he heard from his spies that young Wemyss was trying to drown his anger in beer and curses at the inn which lay at the foot of the castle.

Bothwell lost no time and that very evening he donned a clever disguise and made his way into the tortuous narrow streets near Edinburgh Castle to find the discontended serf. As luck would have it, O'Logie appeared in the inn at just the right time and was only too glad to drink the health of the noble stranger who had joined him at his table.

The two met at the inn several times in the days that followed, and after they had tossed back a good many jugs Wemyss began to feel a friendly disposition towards the unknown guest.

'I do not wish to keep my secret any longer,' he exclaimed and banged the table so hard with his fist that the mugs rattled. Then, lowering his voice he confided to Bothwell how he was getting sick and tired of being in the service of such a swollen-headed King.

The Earl struck while the iron was hot. 'You are not the only one, my friend, who is not fond of James the Sixth,' he said leaning confidentially towards the young man. 'He is hated by a great many other Scots, and they are preparing a plot against him. Do you know that you might be a great help in that undertaking, by merely opening a single door?'

'There's a plan I could go along with!' said Wemyss and he banged the mug on the table so violently that the beer spilled over the edge. 'Which door should it be, if I may be bold enough to ask?'

The Earl explained to Wemyss that it was the door of the King's bedchamber through which the conspirators must enter unobserved.

'When on the agreed night you hear an owl hoot three times,' Bothwell went on, 'the King will be sure to be fast asleep. All that is needed is for you to unlock the door silently and I and three other men will quietly slip inside. We shall take James prisoner and announce in the morning that his reign is at an end. I bet my best horse that both town and castle will greet this news with a thunderous cheer.'

Afterwards the two men parted on the understanding that the next time they would fix the date of the fateful night.

The two were never to meet again however, and suddenly the young Wemyss had all the time in the world to muse over the cause of this. He was sitting in fetters in the dungeon of Edinburgh Castle awaiting his execution.

The fact was that the cautious King James had his spies even in the remote inn under the castle walls. These servants had heard every word even through a dozen doors, and thus were able to inform the ruler in no time that O'Logie and Bothwell were plotting to overthrow him.

The King was furious, 'Just look what our faithful footman has become. He has taken up with my bitterest enemy, and I was fool enough to place such confidence in his honest face!' and he immediately ordered O'Logie to be im-

prisoned in the most secure cell of the castle dungeon. On days when the sun did not shine, all of Edinburgh Castle looked like one vast prison-house; what hope could there be for one who had now become a real prisoner within its walls?

The Earl of Bothwell vanished into the unknown immediately after Wemyss had been arrested. The conspiracy was disclosed, so it was every man for himself. Yet the noble lord of Bothwell did not even think of Squire O'Logie upon whom he had brought so much misery.

On the other hand, Margaret's loving heart was pounding with fear. The maiden knew only too well how strong and thick the prison walls were; she also knew that Wemyss was being guarded by the commander of the castle garrison, Captain Carmichael himself. Now he was the master of the keys of O'Logie's cell and by the King's order he was to keep them upon his person at all times. A rumour soon spread among the servants that the former King's footman had turned out to be a dangerous criminal, but Margaret never wavered in her firm resolve that she would save her beloved from death at the hands of the executioner.

'Wemyss must have had good reason to become involved with such wicked conspirators! Such an honest man would not hurt a fly, let alone the King of Scotland. King James must be a fine one to make Wemyss so cross with him. Let anyone say what he will, my Wemyss is sure to be innocent!'

Margaret was so certain that her idea was the truth that the very next morning when dressing her mistress for breakfast she confessed to her her love for the young squire, and with tears in her eyes begged the Queen to intervene with the King to grant O'Logie his pardon.

'I would very much like to help you, my dear,' said the Queen pityingly. 'But this time the King will not heed my intercession, he is afraid of a conspiracy. You had better go and seek him out yourself, he may take pity on the tears on your beautiful young face!'

Margaret put on her green Sunday best attire, dressed her golden hair into graceful curls, and begged the King to receive her in audience.

'What can I do for my lovely chambermaid?' joked James the Sixth courteously. 'Particularly when she looks so splendid today,' he added with even greater courtesy and twirled his moustaches into fine points. Whereupon he pulled out of his bosom his gold comb inlaid with precious stones to comb down his hair.

Now it happened that one tooth of the comb drove itself under the signet-ring on his hand causing the King such pain that he angrily flung the ring and the comb on to the little table in front of his looking glass.

'You yourself know best, Your Majesty,' Margaret started speaking with a graceful curtsy, 'that a generous deed sometimes brings a ruler more glory than a victory in battle. Grant pardon to my unfortunate O'Logie, and I will promise you that he will never again give you the least of trouble!'

'Oh, and how do you come to know it so positively?' laughed the King.

'I will not let him do it, Your Majesty, it's as simple as that. I will marry him and become a wife whom her husband obeys implicitly.'

'Just see what confidence our chambermaid has in herself!' The King began to laugh heartily, but then his face grew stern and the look he now gave Margaret was suddenly as cold as ice.

'No, my dear, I will not grant pardon to Wemyss O'Logie, not for all the gold in Scotland. He allied himself with rascals who are out to rob me of my throne; I questioned him all day yesterday. Wemyss O'Logie must die!'

The monarch's voice sounded as icy as the look in his eyes. 'No,' thought Margaret, 'this arrogant monarch is not going to yield to my entreaties! Well, then I shall have to do without

your pardon, and you shall be sorry for that; you shall experience shame such as is hard to bear even for an ordinary man, let alone for a ruler. You shall lose your battle, King James, by a woman's wit!'

At that moment the chambermaid was covering her eyes with the palm of her hand, and blindly staggering towards the little table which stood in front of the looking glass as though seeking some support until at last she fell across its top.

'I hope she has not fainted,' thought the King, 'for I have no idea of how to bring round a fainted person! If she does not come to, I will have to call in some help, and this will cause a pretty show!'

However, to the monarch's great relief, the chambermaid came to in a moment and left the chamber with her head up. The King, too, left his study, for it was nearly dinner time. He was perplexed and upset after all that had just happened, so that he quite forgot all about his precious comb and his signet-ring which he had put aside.

The King and Queen greatly enjoyed their dinner. They consumed much fine food and strong wine, so much so that they were nearly overcome by sleep at the table. So they took themselves straight from the dinner table to bed and sank into a deep sleep almost straight away.

Margaret, the chambermaid, however, was bursting with life, for events could not have run smoother. Apart from herself and the sentry who now had to spend the night in the anteroom of the King's bedchamber instead of O'Logie it was probable that no other person in the castle had an inkling of the fact that the King had gone to sleep so early that night.

The person who probably had the least idea of it was Captain Carmichael, the commander

of the guards and the top castle gaoler. Unless he had to he preferred never to go too far from the cell of Wemyss O'Logie.

The castle dungeon was situated deep under the royal chambers and it was to these, the gloomiest, coldest and dampest parts of the whole castle that Margaret, the chambermaid, rushed, almost breaking her neck as she ran down its steep staircases.

'Oh Captain,' she sighed when she at last found herself face to face with Carmichael, 'may I lean on you for a little while? With all the hurry I was in I nearly sprained my ankle!'

Captain Carmichael felt very pleased that he could offer his arm to a maiden as charming as Margaret.

'What on earth is going on, Margaret, that you are gasping for breath? Is it because somebody has done harm to the Queen?'

'Far from it, Captain. All I have to do is to bring before the King as quickly as possible, at

this very moment, Squire O'Logie who is held prisoner in your jail. The King needs to question him still before going to bed. Indeed, His Majesty has conceived a suspicion that this rebellious young man has not disclosed to him everything about the conspiracy. King James must know it this very evening, otherwise he will be unable to sleep! Here, the King has given me this token so that you may not have any doubt that it is he who sent me.'

With these words Margaret put her hand deep into her pocket and pulled from it James's signet-ring and the comb inlaid with precious stones which he always carried with him. It was because of these two things that she feigned the fainting fit in the King's study, and that was

why she collapsed in front of the looking glass. That was the only way she was able to borrow them without the King's knowledge.

No sooner had Captain Carmichael seen the King's ring and comb than he stood to attention and clicked his heels. That was the very comb which the King used to comb his hair at least ten times in an hour, and the ring with which he sealed documents containing his orders.

'I can see His Majesty has truly provided you with proofs direct from his own hands,' he said to the maiden. 'All I can do is to fulfil His Majesty's order and his will.'

As a true soldier, Carmichael was not used to questioning orders received from above, and in his simple soldierly heart he did not have even an inkling of the kind of things to be accomplished by a woman's wit and a woman's guile. So he obediently unlocked the cell as well as Wemyss's fetters, and led the culprit into Margaret's presence. She only just managed to give Wemyss a secret sign that he should look at her like a stranger and just as desperately as before.

She just could not wait to be all alone with Wemyss! The huge castle was already submerged in a sleepy mood that night, and she hoped that they would find some cranny or a forgotten postern whose bolt had rotted through which they might slip out, thence to the port and a ship as quickly as possible, and away from the country of the Scots!

However, the maiden's joy was short-lived

for the Captain suddenly ordered two armed sentinels to escort Wemyss to the King.

'The road to the royal chambers is long and full of forlorn corners. A criminal such as O'Logie may strangle you before you can shout for help; no, my dear, I cannot let you go on your own unprotected,' said he parting with Margaret in all courtesy.

The poor chambermaid had no choice but to make a grateful curtsy even though she felt like doing away with the Captain along with the two hulking great fellows of his, but her anger left her in a moment. Why, she was sure she could manage to dispose of the two pot-bellies who were hard put to it not to stumble over their own halberds whilst wheezing up the narrow winding stairs!

All she needed now was a stroke of a luck: in fact, the forgetful King often failed to lock his study up on leaving. Margaret hoped that today would be no different.

She started urging the three men to a greater hurry up to the floor where the royal chambers were situated. 'Quick, quick, the King is waiting impatiently!'

The march became a trot, and before long the two sentries in heavy armour had sweat pouring from them in profusion, and by the time they reached the King's chambers both were panting like a blacksmith's bellows.

The two fellows were more than pleased to hear Margaret say that His Majesty would not need any guards while questioning Wemyss. They were looking forward to enjoying a spell of undisturbed rest in the corridor. Margaret and Wemyss were in luck, for the King had indeed left his study door open. They entered, and closing the door behind them, fell into each other's arms, but only for an instant. There was still the most important thing to be done: to make haste from the castle before midnight. The sentries were waiting outside, therefore the only way of escape from the chamber was through the window.

Fortunately, the window happened to be at a point in the wall where it was hewn out of a rock so steep that in those parts the palace did not need to be walled in. It was enough to let oneself down to the foot of the rock from where it was not difficult to reach the labyrinth of narrow lanes at the foot of the castle, and there it was easy to escape from any pursuer.

'A rope is what we need: strong enough to hold us both and long enough to reach down to the rock,' whispered Wemyss to Margaret when they had looked down into the moonlit depth.

'How brave he is,' thought the maiden. 'And how much he must love me when he is ready to drop down from such a height with me in his arms!'

'Then we will flee across the sea to my native Denmark,' she smiled at her dearest. 'That blessed plain of fields and meadows stretching from horizon to horizon, full of good harvest and cattle. It will not be difficult for a Scottish squire to farm the rich Danish soil.'

'Just ten fathoms of rope, my darling, and I will sail with you even to the end of the world,' said Wemyss in despair, and at that moment Margaret nearly shouted for joy. For it was only then that she noticed the strong knitted cords hanging at the drawing curtains as well as along the walls, and if these were all to be tied together the length would certainly do!

'But it will not hold both of us,' sighed We-

myss, and Margaret bowed her head in sorrow. She knew she did not possess enough skill or enough strength in her arms to be able to climb down on her own. It did not take her long to recover her smile and good mood.

'Take this,' she said reaching for one of the King's pistols hanging on the wall, 'and stick it into your belt for your defence. And here,' she pulled out a small purse of silver from her deep pocket, 'take this for your sea voyage to Denmark. And wait for me there at the port of Esbjerg.'

However, the young squire would not at first even hear of such a proposal. 'Foolish Margaret, the King is sure to learn first thing in the morning that it was you who helped me escape.'

'Well, the King does not rise so early in the morning,' the maiden replied. 'When you are safe, I will tell the two hulking big fellows in front of the door that the King may go on questioning you deep into the night and send them to have a bit of rest meanwhile. Then, right after dawn when the main gate opens, I will run out nonchalantly with my little bundle pretending that the Queen is sending me on some errand before breakfast. After that I will just try to get by ship to Esbjerg as quickly as possible and will look for you there.'

At last Margaret had been able to offer Wemyss some reassuring words.

'She has not only a loving heart, my dear Margaret,' he thought. 'Even her head is set square on her shoulders, for she has thought of everything in advance. I will do best to obey her in all matters.'

So they fixed the makeshift rope to the lattice of the window frame, and after a fond embrace Wemyss began descending into the darkness.

Foolish Wemyss! He extolled Margaret's prudence, but himself did not show a bit of it. The moment his feet touched firm ground he had no better idea than to fire the King's pistol out of sheer pride about his successful escape.

However, the shot did not escape the fine ear of King James. The sound woke him up right in the middle of a horrible dream about his former footman leading a new conspiracy against him.

'It was no one else but Wemyss O'Logic!' he exclaimed still half dreaming, but it was indeed the truth. He sent for Carmichael who disclosed that O'Logie was out of his cell and that it was Margaret, the Queen's chambermaid, who had led the way. The poor maiden was put behind bars that very night, and patrols were sent out in search of the fugitive to apprehend him and drag him back with the greatest expediency.

'You have indeed an excellent chambermaid, my dear,' King James announced angrily to his wife at breakfast the next morning, and with great indignation he recounted to her all that happened.

The Queen remained silent while he told her the story, and the moment he finished she asked him coldly, 'Where is my first chambermaid now?'

'Down in the prison cell, where Wemyss was confined, my dear. I ordered her to be locked in there and have a good mind to have her beheaded if that blackguard O'Logie is not found within a few days!', whereupon the Queen rose

from the table without a word and left the banqueting hall with an imperious step.

The King did not let this spoil his mood in the least. 'The moment the barber-surgeon arranges my hair, I will descend to the prison cells!' he rubbed his hands and even gave a self-satisfied grin. 'I must put the cursed Margaret through a most thorough questioning. Who knows if she, too, was not implicated in the prepared conspiracy.'

However, when he reached the dungeon, he remained dumbfounded: in Margaret's cell, fettered like a true criminal, sat his own royal spouse too.

'I trust you are not surprised, dear husband,' she said in the quietest voice possible. 'I ordered Carmichael to put me in irons. I belong here just as much as this maiden. She has freed her bridegroom from prison because she loves him. If the plot against you had succeeded and your enemies had put you in prison, God is my witness that I would have tried to help you just the same as Margaret had helped Wemyss. Or is it meet that the Queen of Scotland should love her husband less than her chambermaid his footman?'

King James considered his wife's wise words and then, with a guilty smile, he had Carmichael called in and ordered him to free both women from their fetters without delay. Immediately thereafter he granted Margaret his pardon. All she had to do was to promise she would quit Edinburgh Castle with the greatest dispatch and leave Scotland forever.

The maiden did not mind in the least, of course. She thanked the Queen for her wonderful help, and that very day she embarked at Leith on a ship that was about to set sail for Denmark.

However, her Wemyss did not find it so easy to reach the Leith port. The patrols sent out by the King were busily searching the whole of Edinburgh and its environs, and the youth was forced to use all kinds of intricate dodges to

169

cover his tracks. Even so, he had had some very narrow escapes before he finally reached the Leith quay. What saved him was the gangway of the sailing ship that was just raising anchor prior to sailing. He managed to jump on to it at the very last moment. What a surprise it was for him to meet Margaret who had just embarked on the same ship only a short time before!

When they happily reached Denmark, if we are to believe the verses of the old ballad, they celebrated a merry wedding, and lived happily ever after.

The Black Kitchen at Orava Castle

In the days when Slovakia was part of Hungary, Orava Castle was the seat of the nobleman George Thurzo, one of the wealthiest rulers in the Empire. Because of his coffers full of ducats he was treated with respect by the King of Hungary himself, a fact not to be wondered at, because gold coins were sorely needed by the monarch in order to hold on to his throne.

The fact was that the Hungarian plains along the Danube were under constant attack by the Turks from the South. Riding their fast horses, wielding their sharp sabres, and firing their heavy guns, they never left the King in peace. He was obliged to fight them to make sure that they might not deprive him of his throne one fine day. Of course, all these wars were a very costly business.

Thurzo, the rich lord of Orava Castle, enjoyed the ruler's favour, but this did not help to increase his wealth. It had rather the opposite effect in fact, for gold coins for procuring armaments and maintaining the royal army were literally pouring from Thurzo's treasury. At the same time, in these uncertain times, gold was almost worshipped and was rising in value.

So it happened that various adventurers who decided that it would not be amiss to take advantage of the greed for gold knocked at castle gates. Neither was the proud seat above the valley of the Orava River spared their attentions.

The lord of the castle was brooding over a none too pleasant affair: he was trying to calculate how many ducats he had actually spent on the King's wars; truth to tell, they were none too few. 'Do be quiet down there!' he shouted through the open window of his study at the sentries by the gate, 'and as to the rude vagabond who is thumping at the gate as if the world were afire, do bring him up at once. I will have him cast into the dungeon.'

However, the man who appeared before Thurzo's writing desk a moment later did not look at all like an ill-bred person. Carefully combed black curls formed a kind of halo round his forehead and temples, and there were evil eyes flashing from his exotic sunburnt face.

Also his attire bedecked with pendants and chains showed that the foreigner had come from afar.

'Is it a custom in your country to clamour for a visit with such an ado?' asked George Thurzo sullenly.

'Please forgive, noble master,' bowed the foreigner. 'In my country of Italy this is the usual way of letting people know that the visitor is not just an ordinary man. I am Doctor of the universities of Bologna, Padua and Florence. And from the higher learning establishments in faraway Arabia I was forced to carry away my diplomas on a mule, such a multitude of them had been conferred upon me for my learning. Here is one of them!' Whereupon the foreigner pulled from his bosom a large roll of parchment, and proceeded to open it slowly in front of Thurzo's eyes.

'Such a scrawl is something that any local artist could manage. Do you think that people here in the Slovak mountains cannot draw?' said Thurzo doubtingly on seeing the bizarre symbols. Indeed foreigners, of whom a great many wandered about Slovak castles, turned out to be proper impostors on many an occasion.

The newcomer did not bat an eyelid. 'It is Arabic script, sir, and the document testifies that I am well versed in all the secrets and finesses of the science called alchemy. I know how to turn one metal into another, gold being what I am most interested in: if not directly from iron, then certainly from copper, if I have enough time for my experiments and a laboratory provided with all necessary equipment. If I add my own secret mixture into the retort . . .'

Lord Thurzo was hard put not to jump from

his chair. New gold for his half-empty coffers! And should they not suffice after a time he will have others made. And the King himself keeps alchemists at his court, and he is sure to know why.

The foreigner as though he was reading his thoughts lowered his voice confidentially:

'Kings and Emperors need gold most of all, and that is why my proper place is at their courts. You, sir, are said to be richer than the King of Hungary himself, and the more money one has, the more one is in need of it, that is a well-known truth. Therefore I have come to offer you my services. I trust that my abode at your castle will not be any worse than one at a royal court.'

Such eulogy was more than agreeable to Thurzo's ears. In his eyes the stranger suddenly grew into a man of the world who knew more than he had so far chosen to disclose.

'All right,' he said after a moment of reflection. 'You shall get everything you need to make even purer gold than that from which the Hungarian ducat is coined at the Kremnica Mint. Indeed, ten such ducats you shall draw as your monthly pay; and when I have complemented with your own produce what has been emptied from the coffers through the King's wars, you shall meet with a reward which you will not forget to the end of your days. My people will need a waggon to take it to Italy for you!'

173

It was a very generous offer that the lord of Orava Castle embarked upon, and since otherwise he was an awful niggard, he even began to regret this for a while. If Kings can afford to do this however, why could not he, one of the richest men in Upper Hungary? Was he to appear to the Italian like a poor wretch?

The alchemist was alloted one of the prettiest chambers in the castle to dwell in and a kitchen with a big fireplace for his work. After the room had been equipped with flasks, crucibles, retorts, alembics and lamps according to his drawings and wishes, he drove out all busybodies and firmly locked the door behind him.

After that there was such a stinking smoke and fumes streaming out of the kitchen every other day that whoever happened to be anywhere nearby started coughing, his eyes streaming with tears until he almost fell down.

'As if he were roasting and melting together what he has collected at the rubbish heap,' fretted the servants. Even the grooms would give the workshop a wide berth, and that was saying something.

Nevertheless, one night one of them ventured to look inside, and the very next morning he related to the others:

'I saw the Italian work magic. He waved his arm over an onion-shapped pot and a pillar of flame gushed up to the ceiling! The foreigner is in league with unclean powers!'

'There is nothing to fear, he merely threw in some powder that flames up at once and burns out,' said the blacksmith who had assisted the court alchemist in Vienna when he was young.

From that day on they called the foreigner's workshop 'the Black Kitchen', not only because it was blackened with soot.

'Let him hob-nob with Satan himself,' laughed the lord of the castle. 'As long as he makes what he has promised for me.'

However, it was not granted to Thurzo to look forward in peace and good cheer to the alchemist's gold; for once again the Turks be-

gan to wreak havoc down in Lower Hungary.

So the master of Orava Castle was forced to reach deep into his coffers for coins, muster an army, and set out to the King's aid. Amidst all his cares he did not even find time to go and have a look into the black kitchen to see what progress the alchemist had made in his gold-bearing work.

The foreigner did not seem in any particular hurry now that the lord had departed. His work-shop emitted vapour hardly once in a week, but month after month he continued to draw his ten ducats at Thurzo's behest as before. Indeed, the Italian did not have to go all out to spend the money on his merry excursions; the pay, albeit so generous, was slowly becoming insufficient.

It now seemed as though the devil himself had fixed up matters so that the alchemist's chamber was but a few steps away from the treasury where Thurzo kept his coffers full of gold coins! So one night the clever Italian un-locked the treasury with a skeleton key he had made, and excitedly began to open the lids of the coffers. All he needed to do was to fill a large pouch, and a pretty pile of gold coins was on its way to the cache in the black kitchen.

It was the safest hiding-place for them — for apart from the alchemist no one dared to enter it for fear of the devil's intrigues. The foreigner now had only one big thing to worry about — how to clear out in secret as quickly as possible.

However, not every day is a field day even for imposters, for without warning the lord of the castle returned from a victorious battle against the Turks, and so the dumbfounded alchemist barely had time to rush to the black kitchen and make a proper fire. After all, the master must find him busy working.

Before long, there was Thurzo knocking at the door and saying, 'Sing your praises, my friend, show what it was for that you drew ten ducats month after month. Is the gold you have made fine and genuine?'

'Just a moment, I will open the door for you,

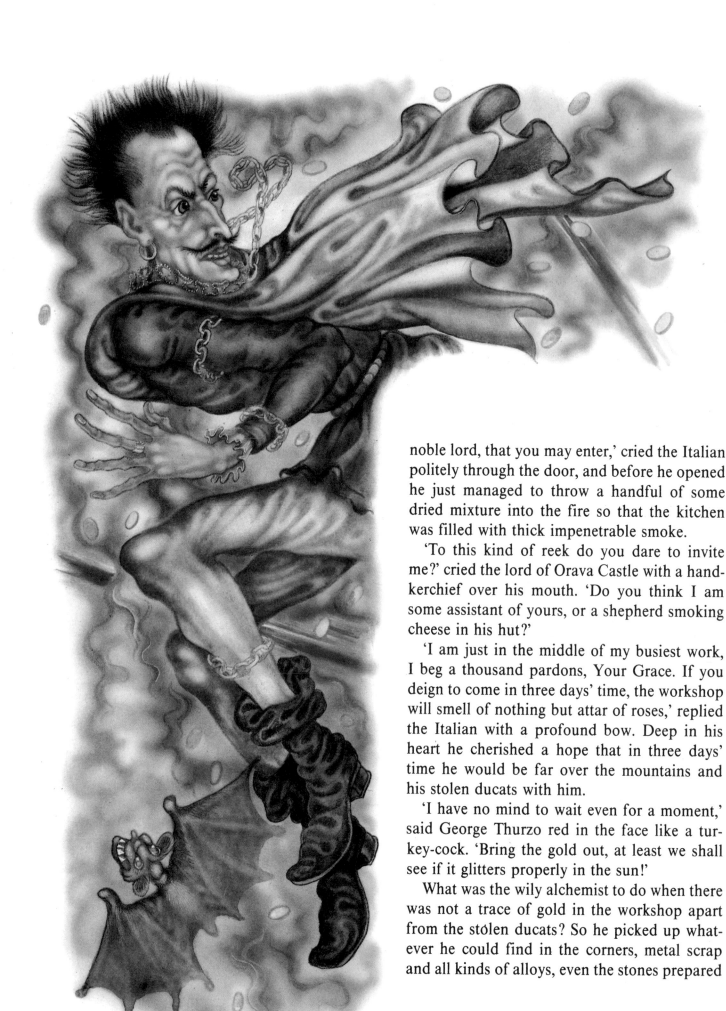

noble lord, that you may enter,' cried the Italian politely through the door, and before he opened he just managed to throw a handful of some dried mixture into the fire so that the kitchen was filled with thick impenetrable smoke.

'To this kind of reek do you dare to invite me?' cried the lord of Orava Castle with a handkerchief over his mouth. 'Do you think I am some assistant of yours, or a shepherd smoking cheese in his hut?'

'I am just in the middle of my busiest work, I beg a thousand pardons, Your Grace. If you deign to come in three days' time, the workshop will smell of nothing but attar of roses,' replied the Italian with a profound bow. Deep in his heart he cherished a hope that in three days' time he would be far over the mountains and his stolen ducats with him.

'I have no mind to wait even for a moment,' said George Thurzo red in the face like a turkey-cock. 'Bring the gold out, at least we shall see if it glitters properly in the sun!'

What was the wily alchemist to do when there was not a trace of gold in the workshop apart from the stolen ducats? So he picked up whatever he could find in the corners, metal scrap and all kinds of alloys, even the stones prepared for lining the fireplace, and started arranging everything in a line in the doorway.

'Is this supposed to be gold?' exclaimed the lord of the castle. 'Is this what I have been paying you for?'

'It is not purified yet, Your Grace! In order to acquire the colour and glitter of precious metal, it must go through its last bath when the moon has waxed into its first quarter and the stars in the sky reach their most favourable conjuction. Then even these grey stones will burst for inside, like the yolk in an egg, the nuggets or purest gold are hidden!'

The lord of Orava Castle listened to the foreigner's rhetoric with growing distrust. He knew something of gold, for his estates contained the gold mines near Banská Bystrica. What could the junk that the grubby fellow had assembled under his feet have to do with gold?

Suddenly Thurzo decided he had had enough of this nonsense and was seized with such rage that he drew his sword from its sheath and pointed it right under the alchemist's chin, crying, 'Enough of this! You shall forfeit your life for your impostures!'

'The game is up,' thought the Italian. 'And what is more, Thurzo does not yet know that the gold in his coffers has dwindled away.'

He sank to his knees and began to beseech the lord in a doleful voice,

'Grant me just one more night, Your Grace! I shall do my best to be ready by the morrow, I will exert myself to the utmost!'

'I shall grant your request; but beware, my friend, unless I have the gold before me by tomorrow morning, I will have you cast down from the highest castle tower!' said the lord of Orava putting his sword back into its sheath.

The foreigner bowed to the ground and disappeared in the black kitchen. There was no thought of escape any longer. His only hope

was to show great industry and expect that the master may take pity on him.

He did not leave the black kitchen even for a moment, and there were clouds of smoke pouring from the chimney and through every chink in the windows. Whoever came nearer could see the alchemist's grotesque shadow flitting behind the windows in the dark-red glow.

The Italian worked as never before. The whole night flames of the queerest shapes and colours lit the kitchen, and whoever would have put his ear to the door or window would have heard bubbling, smacking, hissing and seething of the strangest concoctions and melting metals.

So it went on until cock's crow. At the moment when the first rays of the morning sun bathed the top of the highest tower, a terrific explosion shook the courtyard of Orava Castle.

At once the whole castle seat was alarmed; was it not because the enemy had appeared beneath the walls and was now sending his first greeting from a gun barrel?

When people came running to the servants' hall where the black kitchen used to stand, all they saw was a toppled crucible, otherwise there was nothing to be seen.

After the fresh mountain wind had blown away the blanket of dust which fell down upon the entire courtyard after the explosion, there were some round yellow things to be seen glittering on the paving. Believe it or not, they were ducats of pure gold!

No one would touch them however, even with one finger. 'They come straight from Lucifer,' people whispered. 'Old Nick brought them to the alchemist for having sold his soul to him, and now he has carried him off to hell!'

That was what everyone thought except the lord of the castle. The moment he had a look into his coffers he knew what had happened: those were his own ducats lying in the courtyard scattered by the explosion!

In vain did he send men-at-arms to try and search out the clever impostor, but they always returned empty-handed. Of the alchemist there was not a trace left anywhere.

How Jimmy the Peasant
Was the King of England's Guest

In Northumberland in the north of England there was a King's subject who kept a small homestead. Since this stood on lands belonging to the King he always paid twenty shillings a year in rent to the Royal Treasury, nothing more and nothing less.

Bravely he drove away want from the door of his cottage until his time came to leave this world. When he died it was his son Jimmy who inherited the homestead, nor did he do any worse in husbandry. In fact, the harvest in his fields looked so delectable that it soon disturbed the sleep of the neighbouring farmer, who, at the same time, held the office of the col-

lector of rates and taxes for the Royal Treasury.

'Why should young Jimmy of all people have the lease from the King of such good land when this would better suit myself,' he pondered, tossing and turning in his bed.

So when the date for the payment of Jimmy's rental approached the scheming Treasury offi-

cial told him, 'Our Royal Highness gives you notice. The contract held good only for your father; it cannot be inherited like some utensils or a wardrobe.'

'I will pay forty shillings instead of twenty,' exclaimed Jimmy. 'What shall we live on if I lose the land and the house, since this also stands on royal ground.'

'That's right, my friend, that's right. You will have to move out pretty fast. Go and seek your fortune elsewhere, for doesn't the whole world lie open before you?' rejoined the collector.

'You know I have a wife and small children. Even my old mother works in the fields with us. I just can't wander about the world with them like a tramp.'

The collector was deaf to all his entreaties however. 'In a month the tenancy is over. In a month mind you are out of here!' He turned his back on Jimmy and stalked away with his nose in the air.

'You should take this up with the King,' said his other neighbours. 'After all it is he himself who has rented his own piece of land to your family.'

'I to seek our King?' said Jimmy shaking his head. 'I have never been to see him, and don't feel much like going there.'

However, in the end he begged his mother to give him her blessing, kissed his wife and children, and called to his little dog, 'You shall go to see the King with me, Bow-wow, don't think you'll get out of it!'

Jimmy put on his grey jacket, set a blue cap on his head, grabbed a staff, and he and his dog set off for the south where he had heard London, the royal seat, was supposed to lie.

'How far is it still before we get to our Majesty?' asked Jimmy in the first borough they reached. When he learnt that it was still nine or ten days' proper walk he heaved a sigh at the thought of how much effort and money such a pilgrimage would cost.

'Shouldn't we rather turn back?' he said to

his dog. 'I would know of a better way to spend my shillings and pence than by knocking about inns and paying all kinds of bribes.'

The dog seemed to give him a reproachful look however, and then Jimmy thought of the royal rent collector, took hold of his staff with conviction and stepped out again with a will.

As they travelled their rations were meagre and their nights even worse; well, you get out what you put in. At last, one fine day, the dog sat down in the middle of the road and barked. Jimmy looked into the distance, and what he saw on the horizon was a forest of towers and roofs. It was London! So, in the very first street he enquired about the King and learnt that His Majesty was in London at that very moment, in the Palace of Whitehall. At a nearby inn he found a lodging for himself and his dog, and right after dinner dropped into bed and slept like a log, so tired was he after the journey; he did not wake up until nearly noon the next day.

'Well, our King is sure not to rise right at dawn,' said Jimmy to himself when he finally got up. 'But now we had better get to Whitehall in a hurry.'

'You will find it utterly deserted,' laughed the innkeeper. 'While you were sleeping late His Majesty was pleased to move the whole court to Windsor, a good twenty miles away from here. It's a jolly long walk if you want to get to him for an audience, or whatever you call it.'

'Well, well, isn't it marvellous how his Royal Highness managed to get up so early,' said Jimmy scratching himself behind the ears. 'He will have learnt that I am in London, and made himself scarce; he hasn't got a clear conscience about the lease.'

'To think it's from you of all people that the King would try to flee?' the innkeeper was now laughing his head off. 'Just go and get to Windsor, he is sure to pay you what you deserve!' and he pushed Jimmy out of the door to save himself from choking with laughter.

So Jimmy marched off like a soldier, with his staff over his shoulder and his dog behind him until at last he found himself before the gate of Windsor Castle. It happened to be wide open, but even so Jimmy knocked at it with his stick till the courtyard shook with the blows.

The commander of the guard was dressed up the way only such an officer of His Majesty, the King of England, can be. He shouted at Jimmy whether he was a fool or something to knock at the gate when he saw that it was open. 'And what indeed can we do for you?' he asked.

'Let me talk to my King about my affair,' said Jimmy.

The commander looked at Jimmy's ragged jacket and answered, 'We have enough courtiers here at the castle who can deliver your message to the King, believe me!'

'Oh no, nothing doing. Among the King's grooms I am sure not to find any one whom I would feel like taking into my confidence,' Jimmy shook his head. 'Arrange an audience for me direct with the King. Nor do I want it for nothing, look there is no less than one penny on the palm of my hand all for you!'

'Oh, thank you very much, a whole copper, such a rare thing,' grinned the officer. 'Then I will arrange the audience forthwith.'

He went to the courtyard and whispered into the ear of the first courtier he met, 'There is a dunderhead standing in the gate, a visitor such as has not presented himself for good seven years or more. He calls courtiers the King's grooms and offered me a penny to let him go and see His Majesty himself.'

Even the nobleman in the royal court was

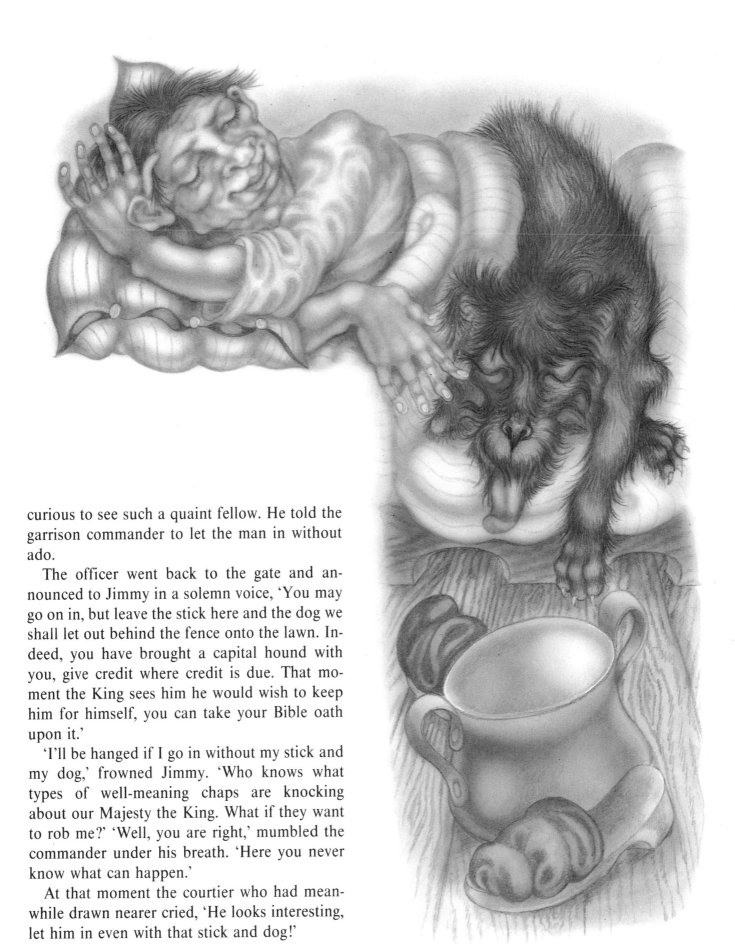

curious to see such a quaint fellow. He told the garrison commander to let the man in without ado.

The officer went back to the gate and announced to Jimmy in a solemn voice, 'You may go on in, but leave the stick here and the dog we shall let out behind the fence onto the lawn. Indeed, you have brought a capital hound with you, give credit where credit is due. That moment the King sees him he would wish to keep him for himself, you can take your Bible oath upon it.'

'I'll be hanged if I go in without my stick and my dog,' frowned Jimmy. 'Who knows what types of well-meaning chaps are knocking about our Majesty the King. What if they want to rob me?' 'Well, you are right,' mumbled the commander under his breath. 'Here you never know what can happen.'

At that moment the courtier who had meanwhile drawn nearer cried, 'He looks interesting, let him in even with that stick and dog!'

'If you really are Your Majesty the King of England, and I do think this is the case, because never in my life have I seen so many tinkling toys round any man's neck,' the good peasant bawled out at the courtier, 'then you are also sure to be the kindest ruler in the world. And if you aren't the King, you are a good man and will surely help me so that I can talk to the King, and I will give you a whole groat for it!'

The courtier was having better fun than at the royal ball, and he said to himself that the fellow might amuse even the King just as well. He asked Jimmy to wait a while, and went to find His Majesty who was trying to amuse himself by playing skittles. When the King heard what the good peasant had already managed to accomplish at Windsor Castle, he exclaimed impatiently,

'Fetch him here with his stick and the dog. He ought to have been here long ago, I am bored stiff with these skittles!'

So the courtier hastened back to the man in the ragged coat, and led him and the dog through all the courtyards, buildings, halls, chambers and ante-chambers that made up Windsor Castle. Jimmy rapped the tiles with his stick wondering why the King was leaving those rooms so unused and did not use them for storing grain and hay for the cattle, until at last they reached the alley where the King and his friends were playing skittles. The King was playing just in his trousers and shirt-sleeves, for it happened to be a hot day.

'So there you are,' said the courtier wiping the sweat off his forehead. 'That is your King over there. Your may go and talk to him.'

'The one in his shirt-sleeves? That's the King you say? Can't you see he has lost even his coat playing those skittles? Damned skittles, is it true they can reduce to poverty even the King of England? A silly game, I don't fancy it.'

However, when the courtier knelt down before the player in his shirt-sleeves Jimmy then believed that the man was really the King, and

told him about his troubles with the collector.

'Have you brought the deed testifying that I have really leased that piece of land to you?'

'That I did, Your Majesty,' said Jimmy pulling the lease from beneath his shirt. 'Now the question is if you can, begging your pardon, read.'

'And if I could not?'

'Well, then I would have to send for my little son to come here. He is only seven, but he can rattle away the letters faster than you would run on the road to save yourself from a runaway mare.'

'I had better spare you the journey, my friend,' smiled the King. He took the paper in his hand, and learnt from it that the family of Jimmy the peasant in Northumberland had the land leased from the King for ever and aye, and as long as he duly paid the rent he must not be given notice.

'How does the family of Jimmy, the peasant from the Northern border, pay its rent?' called the King to his Treasurer. He was able to do so without any trouble, since that dignitary was there playing skittles with him.

So the Treasurer ran off to consult his records and accounts only to report on his return, 'The rent was always paid exactly to a penny and on time.'

'I can see I shall have to send the collector a letter,' the King frowned.

'A letter? Well, you can save yourself the trouble, Majesty. A little letter of sorts can be written cheaply by our scribes in the country.'

'You really are a doubting Thomas, my friend,' exclaimed the King. 'My letter may have some weight, don't you think?'

'Well, if you think so, here is something in advance for your trouble, Your Majesty,' said Jimmy and pulled out a shilling from his pocket.

'No, thanks, no, I really do not need your shilling at all,' protested the King, but all in vain. Jimmy threw the coin inside his shirt.

'Fie, that's cold!' cried the monarch. 'I am all hot from playing that silly game and that shilling of yours has made me shiver all over!'

The King was becoming tired of talking with the peasant. He sent the Treasurer to fetch a pouch with twenty guineas in gold, pressed it into Jimmy's hand and said, 'To pay for your travelling expenses from your home to Windsor and back again, my friend!' Then he whispered into the good peasant's ear: 'First give my paper to your neighbours to read, and only then to the collector, you have my permission. You shall get the letter tomorrow morning, now go and have a little rest and have a good journey tomorrow, Jimmy the peasant!'

Jimmy gripped the pouch with the twenty royal guineas in the palm of his hand as if he were holding his own soul in it. 'Well, I never knew how much money the King had. And on top of that I threw a shilling inside his shirt,' he thought. 'I needn't have pulled it so rashly out of my pocket.'

It was then the duty of the King's servants to take care of Jimmy. After a good dinner he had a proper sleep in a soft bed, and was actually the first man in a peasant's smock shirt who had ever spent the night as a guest at Windsor Castle.

The next day he set off on his way back to his home with his knotted stick over his shoulder, his dog following at his heels, twenty pounds in the pouch, and the King's letter under his cap.

As for reading, Jimmy's neighbours were none the better off than Jimmy himself, but his little son read the letter swiftly, and so they all got to know the King's will and the royal order: Let the collector pay Jimmy the peasant a hundred pounds' indemnity, and unless he does so, let him be bound up and put in fetters.

As luck would have it and the collector happened to be passing by, the neighbours pounced upon him like a flock of wasps, and shut him in the stocks before you could say Jack Robinson. Then they held the King's letter in front of his eyes, and the collector groaned; 'It looks real enough, I recognize the seal!' As he did not wish to sit in the stocks till the evening, let alone overnight, he sent a man to his home to fetch a hundred pounds and immediately paid Jimmy in cash there on the stocks.

The neighbours rejoiced in the courage Jimmy had displayed when he thought nothing of walking through the whole of England from north to south to seek the King himself. Jimmy said to himself that after all this letter was not the same as a letter from the scribe back home in their own county, even though the scribe asked less for one than the shilling that Jimmy had thrown beneath the shirt of His Royal Highness the King of England.

The Three Black Mannikins in the Vault of Salorno Castle

At the Town Hall of the market-town of Salorno high up in the North of Italy visitors would proudly be shown two memorable flasks. The vessels were indeed worth seeing: earthenware with handles and pot-bellied like two fellows who cherish good eating and drinking beyond all treasures. If it were not for their extremely thin and long necks they might have been called jugs.

They looked decidedly old, as was evidenced in the story that the Salorno people told about them.

One day, at a time now almost beyond recall, one honourable Salorno burgher by the name of Christopher Clumsy was returning home from some errand. The summer sun was shining so bright that it lent a gentle appearance even to the castle ruin before the town which Christopher happened to be passing.

'I think I'll have a look up there and see for myself what it really looks like,' said Christopher Clumsy to himself and the next moment he was climbing up the shrubby hillside towards the walls. They were in ruins, and it was not much trouble to climb over them up to the site where the residence of the lord of the castle once stood.

As the oafish burgher looked all around his eyes lit upon some stairs which led deep down under the earth. The bright sun lighted the way all down the well-preserved stone stairs which were as clean as if they had only just been swept a short while before.

That was very odd: who would need to tidy an old ruin? 'Only a pole-cat with his tail,' laughed Christopher. 'But since the steps are so

well kept we shall go and have a look where they lead to.'

Down below he came up against a metal-sheathed door. He gripped the handle. It was smooth as if it had been freshly polished. The heavy oak door opened without a single grating sound, almost by itself.

Beyond the door the steps continued their descent lower and lower, until Christopher suddenly gasped in amazement. The sun's light pouring in through the wickets near the ceiling lit up an immense underground vault. It was not empty. Two rows of enormous barrels lay opposite each other. Eighteen of the giant casks were counted by Christopher Clumsy. Each of them had a brightly polished tap protruding from it, just waiting to be turned. So that was what Christopher did, and from the tap as if it had

been waiting heaven knows how long a golden-bright stream of fragrant potion rushed out, aged smooth and thick as oil. Christopher took a sip from his palm. Never in his life had he drunk such excellent wine! That moment he thought of his wife and his daughter who was nearly old enough to be married. They too must taste some of it, when he got home!

He ran up the steps and out of the ruin and hastened to the town to buy some vessels into which the dainty potion might be tapped. He chose bottles with handles so that they might be carried like jugs; where good drink was concerned Christopher Clumsy did not indeed conduct himself in keeping with his name, nor did he forget to bring a funnel!

Within an hour he was back again at the barrels, and the moment the bottles were full he

Sitting at the table on three little stools were three mannikins wearing cone-shaped black hats, black jackets with red lapels of the kind that is worn here with the local national costume, solid black shoes with silver buckles and thick black woollen stockings. The middle one, who had the longest beard of all the three, fixed Christopher with his black eyes.

The poor burgher nearly sank to his knees with terror. How could they have appeared so suddenly? And where did they come from?

'Did you find the Salorno Castle wine to your taste, Christopher?' inquired the mannikin gravely as though they were in a courtroom.

'Strangely enough, they do look like judges, and even know me by name!' he thought and his poor little soul trembled inside him like an aspen leaf. 'Do they perhaps sit in court over those who have forfeited their lives?' and unwit-

hurried up to the steps. He himself did not know why he should be in such a hurry. Indeed, neither the ruin nor the forgotten barrels had had any master for a long time. 'And if there is no master, then I am no thief,' he reasoned within himself. 'So why am I on the run when there is no one to run away from?' he finally laughed aloud.

'To run away from?' someone repeated after him! It was the echo from the vaulted ceiling but Christopher did not realize this. He turned around in alarm to see who was calling him, and had to rub his eyes to make sure that he was not dreaming.

In front of the steps, where only a little while before a stone floor glittered with moisture, there was a small table with a black tablet on it and something written on it in chalk.

tingly he searched with his eyes the dark corner behind the odd little figures to see if he could see the hangman's red cape in the darkness.

'I did, Your Honour, I did indeed, surely not even the angels in heaven drink a better nectar than this,' mumbled Christopher in all humility, and now he actually dropped to his knees in earnest with fear and anxiety.

'You are well-known all over Salorno and elsewhere as an admirer of good wine, and that you probably would not hesitate to embrace the thief's trade for a good goblet. Am I not right, Your Honours?' said the mannikin slowly turning first to one judge and then to the other with an expression so solemn that it made Christopher's heart pound in his very throat.

'I beg a thousand pardons!' he cried dolefully. 'I did not know that the wine might be somebody's property in such a ruin, most distinguished gentlemen!'

'You call the vault a ruin, do you?' said the mannikin severely. 'Your whole house in Salorno up to the very roof would get lost in its walls. Even a whole street of such houses the vault of Salorno Castle would hide from the world, maybe even the whole of Salorno!'

'Oh, I meant no offence to your most gracious vault!' cried Christopher Clumsy plaintively. 'And as to these flasks, I meant to carry them away not for my sweet tooth, but to give both my wife and daughter the pleasure of tasting such excellent wine. Let them enjoy at least

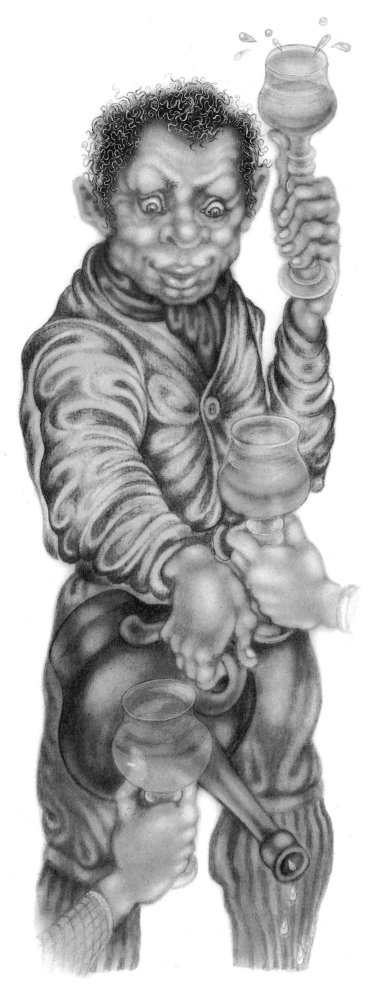

a draught of such rare potion, for they have not exactly a joyful life of it living with me! For be pleased to know, gentlemen, that such an oaf and clumsy clot is not to be found anywhere under the Alps!'

After these words the mannikins' faces became a little kinder. They put their heads together and began taking counsel in silence.

'All right, Christopher,' said the middle one at last. 'As we can see, in matters of wine you are a careful husband and father. From this time on you may come here and tap as much wine into your two flasks as you will need, but listen carefully. This wine may be used only by yourself and the people in your house, and nobody else! To no one else shall you offer a single draught, or disclose with a single word what you have seen here. Should you disregard this warning you will never again be able to show your face here, for you would be made most unwelcome!'

Then the mannikin pointed to the flasks. 'How much do you think they hold, Christopher?' he inquired.

'About one-eighth of a hogshead both together, no more than that,' was Christopher's prompt reply and the mannikins shook their heads contentedly. One of them wrote down something on the tablet, and immediately after that the three judges and all the rest vanished in the dark like a vision.

In the end, like one in a dream, Christopher picked up the flasks from the ground, ascended slowly to the light of day, and dazed from the past events reached his home at last.

The mannikins had vanished, but the wine in the flasks kept its full fragrance and strength. His wife, daughter and all the people living in Clumsy's house enjoyed the wine so much that in a few days the flasks were quite empty.

Before long poor silly Christopher set out for the castle with his flasks for a second time. Once again the stairs were swept clean, the door swung smoothly open at a single touch of his

hand, and just as easy was it to turn the tap on the barrel. He filled the flasks with the golden-bright potion till it flowed down their necks, and set out on his return journey as quickly as possible. Only when he reached the top did he remember that this time there was not a trace of the black mannikins anywhere in the vault.

So it went on for the whole summer, and Christopher as well as all the people in his house seemed to find the wine got better the more they drank of it.

'Until our dying days shall we not exhaust the castle barrels; it might he enough for the whole town!' Christopher would say with pride, and felt more and more like its owner hardly giving a thought to the mannikins in their black clothes.

There is a time for everything however, as the saying goes, and one hot day three friends from the neighbourhood came to see Christopher. They were never particularly fond of Christopher, but now that he and his whole family enjoyed good wine under the garden bower from full glasses day after day and turned their eyes to the sky with delight, they could not sleep for envy or wrath.

'The sun is scorching hot today,' they said standing in Christopher's doorway wiping the sweat from their foreheads. 'Before we crossed the street, our throats were dry with thirst.'

'For that I have here a capital medicine: you shall see for yourselves,' exlaimed Christopher by way of welcome. Swollen with pride, he quite forgot what the three mannikins in the castle vault had impressed upon him, and he started pouring out the wine for his guests as though it were a christening party.

'What sparkling wine you've got, Christopher,' they fell to praising after the very first draught. 'Where do you buy it? We would also like to go and fetch some.'

Christopher only pushed his thumbs beneath his belt, saying, 'I won't tell. That's my secret.'

'It can't be otherwise, Christopher must be

stealing it from somebody's cellar. Such rare wine is not to be bought from any mere merchant. He will keep it like the apple of his eye for himself or for his offspring. The older the wine, the better!' his neighbours predicted.

'What about denouncing burgher Clumsy at the town hall for thieving,' said the one who was most annoyed with Christopher. The other two nodded approval, and since nowhere takes very long to get to in Salorno, and hence not the town hall either, they set off there.

A few days later the city fathers, headed by the mayor, summoned Christopher Clumsy for a thorough questioning. Salorno wine enjoyed great reputation and to steal it was not just an ordinary theft.

'First of all go and fetch the flasks that hold the wine,' ordered the mayor, 'so that we can have a look at the exhibit.'

They performed their duty very well; and were so thorough that it was not long before they could see the very bottoms of the flasks.

'Well,' said the mayor having wiped his moustache after finishing the last draught. 'Christopher, this is wine that you could not have stolen from any local wine merchant. Within my memory we have never bottled such an excellent potion from the local vineyards. If you own where it comes from you shall be free.'

Christopher Clumsy was scared stiff of jail, for he had been shut up there when thanks to his clumsiness in some throng he knocked down the mayor's wife. So after a brief hesitation he gave away everything that had happened in the cavern beneath the castle ruin. He did not even hold back about the tablet on the little table, let alone the three black mannikins and the barrels with the taps.

'You have uncommon luck, Christopher. The spirits of Salorno Castle have bestowed their favour on you,' said the mayor. 'Although the ruin had been searched thoroughly none of the rest of us has ever come across any stairs leading to a vault, let alone across any barrels.'

With this the interrogation ended. Christopher Clumsy was set free but on one condition: that at the very next day's sitting of the town council he would bring the flasks refilled with the extremely rare gift of the Salorno Castle hogsheads.

Christopher was getting ready to go to the castle as if he were pulled by two and pressed by four. The mannikins' warning not to tap for anyone but himself and his family came to life in his head with all its urgency and weight. He seized the flasks however and set off for the ruin even before the evening fell, saying, 'I had better have done with it!'

Once at the castle he directed his steps, as usual, straight to the steps leading underground, but what a surprise! Where they had been there was just rubble overgrown with bur so it was a wonder he did not break his legs in that pile of stones.

'I must have lost my way,' he said to himself after stumbling in vain here and there for quite a while. It was indeed no easy matter to search amidst the broken masonry. Christopher no longer felt his knees for the pain. His clothes were in tatters, and still there was no trace of the steps. When it grew completely dark, he sat down exhausted and in despair on a small tumbled granite pillar. There was no rest to be granted to Christopher Clumsy that night however!

Like a sudden hail such slaps and blows converged on him from all sides that he hardly knew which of them to dodge first, and the worst of it was that those who dealt them were not at all to be seen, although a full moon had just risen and its white light lit up every little stone all around.

So powerful were the blows Christopher Clumsy had collected from the invisible fists that he lay on the ground for a long while like a dead man. Then after recovering a little, he suddenly spotted a ray of light coming out of a crevice. He crawled on his knees as far as the opening and looked inside, and there, wonder of wonders, in the depths below him he saw the familiar vault with the barrels of wine and the three mannikins sitting at their little table!

In the light of the lantern, for this was the light that penetrated through the crevice, they were writing something with chalk on the tablet before them. Now and then they put their heads together so as to consult: it looked as if they were counting something important. In the end the middle one made two resolute strokes on the tablet.

When he had stood it against the wall and placed the lantern by it, Christopher saw a bold

cross. The death cross, the one that is painted on the gate of the man who has been picked out as a victim of vendetta.

A terrified shudder ran through Christopher's aching body. He could not tear his eyes from the tablet for a long time even though the ones who had written on it had vanished in the dark of the vault some time before. Only the strokes of the tower clock at Salorno returned Christopher to life, it was striking eleven.

'In the end I shall be overtaken here by the hour of phantoms,' he thought with a shiver running down his spine. 'Quick, away from here. I'd rather sit in jail until Advent time than stay in this place!'

He dropped the flasks, forgot all about the pains inflicted by the invisible thrashing, and began to climb down the rubble away from the castle as fast as his legs would carry him.

He breathed a heavy sigh of relief when he finally landed on the hillside above the township with the castle far behind him. The whole of Salorno with all its houses and lanes lay open before him, clearly visible in the light of the full moon. He even spotted his own house, but what strange carriage was that standing before the entrance? It had just begun to move, with its followers filling the whole street.

Christopher Clumsy remained transfixed as if thunderstruck. The mysterious procession travelled out of the town and was slowly approaching the hillside where he was sitting. He knew that unless the moon hid behind the clouds he would see more before long, and so he did, for the carriage was a black hearse with a coffin inside! Behind it walked the priest and his acolyte with a little cross on a long pole, and behind those two, Christopher's eyes popped out till they nearly fell out of their sockets, walked his own wife and daughter in tears as the mourning next of kin! Then at a distance the distinguished burghers from the neighbourhood as well as friends from further afield, and moaning maid-servants. There was no doubt any longer, he was watching his own funeral, for it was he, Christopher Clumsy, being driven in that coffin.

At that moment, midnight was striking at the Salorno clock-tower. A black cloud passed across the moon, everything sank into darkness, and Christopher began to lose consciousness and he swooned at the horrendous sight, and rolled down the hillside like a bale of beans.

Only the fresh morning breeze from the mountains brought him round and no sooner had he got to his feet than he rushed home as fast as his legs could carry him, swearing a solemn oath: he would never put his foot on Salorno ruin again, as long as he lived.

Everyone in Christopher's household was happy to be done with the wine, but the city fathers just would not have it. Only when they sent the town clerk to the castle, and he found two earthenware flasks sticking out of a deep crevice did they come to believe him.

So it was that Christopher Clumsy gained his freedom, and the two wine flasks found their place on the mantelpiece of the Town Hall fireplace as a reminder of the three black mannikins who had appeared to Christopher Clumsy in the vault of Salorno Castle.

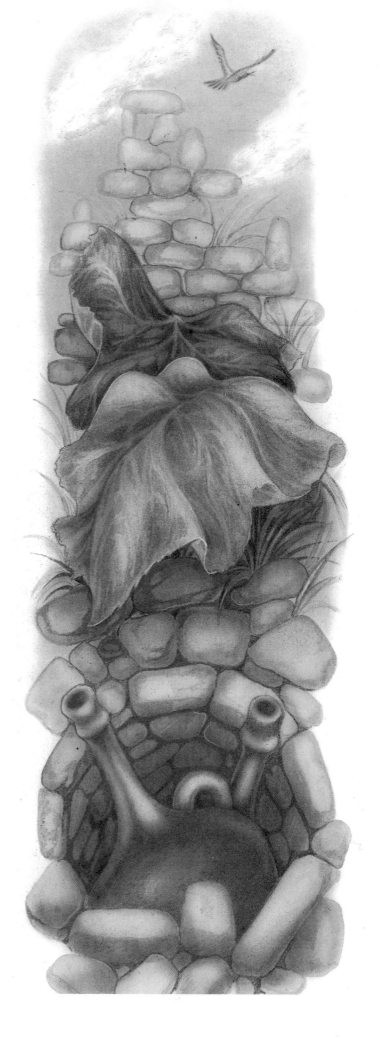

The Treasure of the King of Sorbia

Once upon a time the Sorbs had a mighty King ruling over them. However, in one great battle he is said to have been routed and to have been deprived of all he possessed. He lost his army and all his power, and fled with just a handful of faithful followers to avoid capture by the enemy.

He did not stop before he reached Spreewald, a wide wild mead forest overgrown with wild bulrush, hops and mistletoe. The River Spree flowed through the wasteland by way of a complex network of arms and tributaries. Instead of paths and roads water flooded the countryside under the vaults of ancient trees, and marshes and quagmires threatened the traveller at every step. Even the animals found it hard going to roam about the region, let alone pursuers in heavy armour. The King could feel secure.

He chose a nearby knoll which later came to be called Schlossberg, Castle Hill, had a small castle built on the site, and settled there. That forest retreat recalled rather a robbers' den than a king's seat: it was said that in building it the King had had the help of the devil himself.

Anxious thoughts about his enemy did not leave the beaten ruler even in these parts. Just to make sure, he had his horses shod the other way round: so his tracks would run in the direction opposite to the one in which he was travelling. Also, even if the foe should happen to penetrate as far as these remote parts he was protected by a magic bridge which was also rumoured to be a gift from the devil. It would appear before the King above the marshes and the streams only to vanish again as soon as he had ridden across it.

After a time the King married, and looked forward to an heir. However, children just would not come, and then the devil who never gives anything for nothing inspired the royal couple with the idea of committing a heinous crime.

Not far from the castle there was a woodcutter living in a forest shanty with his wife and

a little son and daughter. The boy was deft and bright, the little girl tender and as pretty as a picture. The King and Queen had taken a fancy to them a long time before. So the Queen persuaded her spouse to murder the woodman and his wife in secret, and then adopt their children.

However, just as they had resolved to do the deed, they were overtaken while on a journey by a tempest the like of which no one in the whole county ever remembered. In the gusts of the gale wind trees were torn out at the roots and the clouds were ripped apart by jagged blue lightning, and the torrents that sprang from them caused the river to overflow its banks.

The King and Queen were hard put to it to turn their horses and return to the castle. Nor did they enjoy safety for long. A bolt of lightning so powerful and bright that it turned the sky into a fiery furnace cleaved the structure in two, and the castle together with its inhabitants caved in and sank into the earth.

In the spot where the fiery whip pierced the earth a black hole has remained ever since. It is so deep that a stone thrown down it will seem to fall for an age before the sound of it hitting the bottom rings out. As a result of this, a story went about for centuries that the lightning had struck down even the King's strong-box full of gold coins, and there were many whose greed drove them to try and get at the treasure.

Those of a braver ilk let themselves down on a rope as though into a well, but not even half way down they tugged at the rope as a sign that they wanted to be pulled up again. They said once in the depths of that devilish cavern they had a feeling as if a dead man's bony hand was reaching out for them.

Only one traveller, a miller who learned about the King's treasure in a mill, is said to

have held out all the way down to the bottom. No wonder, he had fortified himself thoroughly in advance with a bottle of brandy.

Well, they pulled him up again after some time, without the treasure, but with an incredible story. This is what he said.

'It is exceedingly light down there, like under a chandelier somewhere in a castle saloon; and four painted doors lead to the four points of the globe and have gold mounting and handles. Upon each of the thresholds lies a coiled snake with a body as thick as a pillar. I had no other idea than that the monsters were fast asleep, but the moment I stepped out towards one of the doors the snakes lifted their heads and started pouring forth such hissing and whipping out of their tongues at me so vehemently that I was fain to tug at the rope to be pulled up again.'

The neighbours shook their heads, but what they really thought was, 'Is it not the hard stuff talking out of you, dear fellow, that you had drunk to fortify your guts?'

Be that as it may, when he had told his story, any further treasure-seekers were all but discouraged from letting themselves down into the bowels of the Earth.

Well, it is the usual story. Fortune often favours the one who does not go after it. One fine day there was a merry soldier marching along the road that led past the knoll. He stepped along briskly to the rhythm of a song, for he was going home on a furlough!

Towards noon the sun became scorchingly hot and the soldier's knapsack weighed down heavily on his back so he began to look around for a place where he could rest in the shade.

As he was looking round about the road he suddenly became aware that there was someone down at his legs stepping out along with him. He immediately pinched the lobe of his ear to make sure he was not dreaming, for the mannikin with pointed goatee and a face plump and round like a melon barely reached half way up his calves!

'Where are you off to, dragoon Makarits,' he asked the soldier as if they had known each other all their lives.

'Where do you know my name from?' stammered the soldier dumbfounded.

'I know even more,' laughed the Dwarf. 'You are going to see your parents who live in poverty in their hut, and you would like to bring them something substantial to improve their lot; but there are only miserable groats clattering in your pocket.'

'You are right,' sighed Makarits. 'A soldier like myself is poorer than a churchmouse.'

'Well, but today is your lucky day,' said the mannikin. 'You can have a pretty pile of gold coins if you wish.'

'Gold coins?' exclaimed the soldier. 'I like that!'

'If you walk up that knoll over there,' said the mannikin pointing to the Castle Hill, 'you will find a little cave in the middle of the hillside. Inside, there is an old grey hag sitting behind a spinning wheel and spinning like mad. In the wall behind her opens a passage leading to the treasure. Just go in without any ado; at the end of it are three big piles of gold coins.'

'Well, and what have I done to deserve such good fortune?' asked the soldier all of a sudden wrinkling his brow. As a soldier he was used to all kinds of ruses and he had better take care not to fall into the Dwarf's trap.

'Perhaps because you are of a merry disposition and make little of your misery. I am fond of such fellows,' laughed the Dwarf, but then he said with a grave face, 'Don't tell me, dragoon Makarits, that you are frightened after all.

A pretty soldier, that you are! Listen carefully to what I am going to tell you now. From each pile take only three handfuls of gold — that's all your knapsack will hold anyway. The old woman will try to persuade you to take everything, but don't listen to her. She is doomed to spin at the spinning wheel until the treasure disappears from Castle Hill. If you were responsible for this, you would have to sit down at the spinning wheel in her stead and spin for ever and ever whether you be a king or a dragoon!'

'No, thanks,' cried Makarits. 'To spin like a woman and in a soldier outfit on top of that!'

'If you do as I have advised you, you shall become rich,' said the mannikin.

'I should like to repay you somehow,' said the soldier scratching his ear, 'only I have nothing to offer.'

'How do you mean you have nothing? It will be enough if you lend me your dragoon's sabre for a while.'

'What good will it be to you?' smiled Makarits to himself. 'For it is twice as long as you are!' But he drew the sabre out of its sheath in all seriousness, and bowed down to hand it over to the Dwarf.

All at once he nearly turned a backward somersault with alarm, for the Dwarf gripped the weapon with the strength of a giant, and jumping aside swung it over his head until it whizzed through the air.

'I have some business down there, and it will be a big battle and a lot of fighting,' he said pointing at a body of water which could just as well have been a dead arm of the river Spree as a pond.

Deep down at the bottom was the lair of an evil water-sprite but the soldier had no knowledge of this.

'I will now jump down and you pay good heed,' the Dwarf went on. 'When the surface settles down again bubbles will rise, perhaps for a long time after, perhaps for just a brief moment. If they are white it will be a sign that

I have carried the day, but if their colour is that of blood, then you should know I have lost, Makarits, and take care you get away from here as quickly as possible!'

Saying this, the Dwarf swung the sabre once more, and then he plunged into the water.

The soldier did not have to wait long, for soon the surface became decked with dazzling bubbles as white as fresh snowflakes, and soon after that the Dwarf swung back up on to the bank with a tender little red-haired maiden in his arms.

'So I have beaten the water-sprite!' he whooped with delight. 'He was holding this poor water nymph in prison. She had to keep house in his untidy den of reeds instead of dancing merrily up on the clearing with her companions. Only the weapon of an honourable man was good enough to deal with the water-sprite. I could not but help to believe in your honesty, and for this you deserve the gold of the Sorbian King.'

They parted beneath a spreading linden-tree and the soldier stepped out up to Castle Hill. There he found everything as the Dwarf had told him: a cave half way in the hillside, inside it an old woman spinning on a spinning wheel, as well as the passage in the wall behind her which led him all the way to a vaulted cave with an opening in the ceiling through which the light shone. He saw gold coins arranged into three piles so bright his eyes were dazzled with the shine. He did not linger. Acting on the Dwarf's advice, he took only three handfuls from each pile, not a whiff more.

'Well, why are you so modest, soldier? A lad like you must carry off such three piles on his shoulders like a feather. I will lend you a sack for them. Just go and take them all, or tomorrow they may be pecked by another blackbird.'

That was what the old hag was shouting down the passage using a long pole to push towards Makarits a very long sack of such a size that it could have held nearly a whole house.

Makarits did not seem to see or hear her. He clambered back through the tunnel pushing the knapsack which carried gold coins before him like a shield. The moment he crawled out he set the knapsack on his back, ran down Castle Hill, and went upon his way.

The old woman sighed and once again sat down at her spinning wheel.

'I hope the time may come when a grasping fellow comes along who will want to carry away the whole treasure,' she muttered angrily.

As it was the old woman in her enchantment had already been spinning there for centuries. Indeed, it was she who all that time before had succumbed to the devil's wishes and persuaded her husband, the King of Sorbia, to contemplate a crime which thanks only to the elements of Nature could not be carried out.